Readers love ANDREW GREY

A Serving of Love

"…delightful characters to root for and a romance that will leave you aching for more."

—Love Romances & More

Love Means… No Fear

"I would recommend this story to anyone looking for romance. I also found this series to be a lovely introduction to m/m erotica."

—The Romance Studio

Accompanied by a Waltz

"A story about first love, loss, and the rediscovery of love all wrapped up in its pages."

—Fallen Angel Reviews

A Troubled Range

"…Andrew Grey delivers a solid, sweetly romantic, and delightful story that will leave you clamoring for more after the last page is read."

— Love Romances & More

The Best Revenge

"…one of the most romantic and heartwarming stories I've read."

—Man Oh Man Reviews

http://www.dreamspinnerpress.com

ARTISTIC

Pursuits

ANDREW GREY

Dreamspinner Press

Published by
Dreamspinner Press
4760 Preston Road
Suite 244-149
Frisco, TX 75034
http://www.dreamspinnerpress.com/

Artistic Pursuits

Cover Art by Anne Cain   annecain.art@gmail.com
Cover Design by Mara McKennen

ISBN: 978-1-61372-367-8

Printed in the United States of America
First Edition
February 2012

eBook edition available
eBook ISBN: 978-1-61372-368-5

To Jane,
one of my incredible editors,
for giving me the idea for this story.

PROLOGUE

"MORNING, Mr. Temple," a child on the sidewalk called and waved, and he waved back through the open car window before turning off Prospect Avenue and into the parking lot of the Milwaukee Conservatory of Music. Parking in his reserved spot with its small sign that the faculty had gotten him for Christmas, Jerry smiled and turned off the local classical music station before rolling up his car windows and turning off the engine. Once out of the car, Jerry walked across the lot and around to the front of what he considered to be one of the most amazing buildings in town. Still carrying his briefcase and coffee, but no longer really paying much attention to either, Jerry walked around the side of the building and stood looking at what had once been the round conservatory of the grand mansion that served as the music school's home, and now served as their performance space.

"It's a wonderful thing you did."

Jerry turned and saw an old, elegantly dressed woman standing behind him. "Excuse me?" he said politely.

She turned and pointed to one of the high-rise buildings that surrounded them. "I live up there. Damned retirement community full of—" She paused and shuddered slightly. "—old people who do nothing but sit around and fart their lives away. My apartment has a view of your building, and I watched as you did all those wonderful restorations. It's a good thing you did, to save this building. I remember coming here once as a child."

"Were you here when the Marsons owned it?" Jerry asked, and he saw her nod before smiling at him and continuing on her morning walk. "Have a good day, ma'am."

She turned and gave him another smile. "You too, young man," she answered before continuing down the sidewalk. Jerry turned his attention back to the building. He'd never thought that a building could become so important to him, but this one certainly had. Built at a time when the Milwaukee lakefront had been lined with grand homes like this for miles, this was one of few that remained in all of downtown, and the only one right on the bluff overlooking Lake Michigan. When he'd been offered the post of executive director four years before, he almost hadn't taken the job because the facilities at the school were in such bad shape. The mansion had fallen into disrepair from years of use and too little maintenance. Jerry's first order of business, after reviewing the curriculum, had been to put together detailed architectural and decorative plans to renovate and restore the building. That had turned out to be the easy part. The hard part had been how to pay the multimillion-dollar price tag.

Jerry cringed as he remembered standing in front of the board to present his plan. "We all agree," the board chairman had said, "something must be done, but how do we pay for it?" He'd looked to the other board members, and they all had the same look of resignation. "I suppose we'll have to sell the windows." Heads bobbed, and a look of sadness came over each and every board member. One of the highlights of the once-grand mansion was a set of three large Tiffany "dogwood" windows that decorated the landing of the main staircase. They were stunning, and it had nearly broken Jerry's heart, as well as the board's, to think of selling.

"I hope it doesn't come to that," Jerry had answered. "I took the liberty of calling the *Milwaukee Journal,* and they have agreed to do an article on our plans for the renovations. With your permission, I'd like to share our plans with them as well as our plight. I'm hoping that somehow we can raise the money we need without selling the windows. I'd like to ask that we hold off on a decision for a few months."

The board had agreed, the newspaper article had led to a television interview, and the money began to flow in. What had surprised everyone, including Jerry, was that while they got some large contributions, they also got many, many small donations from ordinary people throughout town, people who had never had a connection to the school, but who wanted to help save the windows. Within a few months, they had the money to begin work, and within a year, they'd reached their goal. And Jerry had remained front and center in their campaign to "Save the Tiffanys." At the completion of the renovations, the newspaper had done a long article on the entire saga, as well as some of the things they'd found while doing the work, such as an incredible hand-blown chandelier inside a boarded-up fireplace.

At the unveiling, the conservatory had invited all the donors, big and small, to an open house, and thousands of people had shown up. Jerry and his staff had spent the entire day proudly giving tours of the building that concluded with a trip up the staircase to see the windows that they'd not only helped to save, but had given enough money that the conservatory had been able to have the windows themselves restored and strengthened as part of the renovation. That day had been one of the most amazing and incredible days of Jerry's life.

Turning away from the building, Jerry's thoughts turned back to the day's work. Walking back around to the front of the building, Jerry listened to the birds for a second before setting down his case and unlocking the front door. He deactivated the alarm before pushing the door open. Students were already arriving behind him, and Jerry said good morning as he picked up his leather case of papers and led the way inside.

As he did every morning, Jerry walked to the base of the stairs and gazed upward. But this morning, instead of light blues, rich whites tinged with pink, and long brown and black branches with delicate dogwood blossoms clinging to them, all he saw was the sky outside. Jerry stood stock still as first his case and then his cup of coffee hit the shining parquet floor.

CHAPTER 1

A FILE whacked harder than necessary on his desk, and Franklin looked up from where he was filling out a report. "Try not to screw up this one too badly," his supervisor said without a hint of his usual humor, and Franklin knew exactly why. His last assignment hadn't gone exactly according to plan, and one of the men on the team had been shot. Franklin took a deep breath and stopped himself from lashing out at the man the way every fiber in his being urged him to. What happened hadn't been his fault, and Franklin knew it, as did everyone else, but that didn't seem to matter—they needed someone to blame, and he was it.

"Nice show of support," Franklin muttered under his breath. As the junior member of the team, he knew he was going to take crap for everything that happened, but he didn't have to like it.

"Hey!" Harvey, his supervisor, snapped, leaning close to him. "We all know you got bad information, but you messed up because you didn't double-check the address on your way over. You could have and should have. Because you went to the wrong house first, you lost the element of surprise, and Stevens got shot. You were in charge of the operation because you asked to be, so you take the lumps." Harvey's expression softened a little. "Everyone messes up; it'll pass."

"Yeah, but not everyone messes up and gets someone shot," Frank retorted, and that was the heart of the issue. Frank knew he'd made a mistake, one that could have cost someone their life. Stevens didn't blame him, but everyone else did, and more importantly, he blamed himself.

"So make up for it with this one," Harvey told him before turning and walking into his glass-walled office near the corner. Frank opened the folder and began to read. As he did, he wondered why Milwaukee PD had turned this case over to the FBI. It seemed like a simple theft. Persons unknown had stolen a set of valuable windows from the Milwaukee Conservatory of Music. Sure, the items stolen had been valuable, but that didn't warrant an investigation by federal agents.

"Don't go to the wrong house this time," Martinson taunted as he passed Frank's desk.

"Thanks, Martinson. Don't trip over your own feet," Frank retorted with little humor. He'd be damned if he was taking flak from the department geek. Yes, he'd made a mistake, but Martinson was a total fool, and Frank couldn't figure out why he was still around except that the man was great with numbers and computers, just not people. Martinson continued on his way, completely unfazed, and Frank watched as Martinson nearly fell into his chair, then looked at the floor, probably trying to figure out what he'd tripped over.

"Frank," Harvey called from his office, "you finish reading that case file?"

"Yes." Frank got up and walked into Harvey's office. "Why'd this get bumped to us? Looks like a straightforward theft." Frank stood in front of Harvey's desk. He hadn't been invited to sit, and no one sat in Harvey's office unless invited.

"If it were, we wouldn't have the case," Harvey said, staring at Frank, waiting for him to continue. "So...."

Frank fidgeted slightly, knowing there was something he was missing, and it pissed him off. "There must be more to it. I saw the reports about this theft a few days ago. These windows are worth millions, but shit... who's going to buy them? They have to be nearly impossible to sell. You think they were stolen to order?"

"That's what you need to find out. I need you to get down there right away. The reason we've been called in is because this is bigger than a simple theft, or at least MPD and Interpol think so. Interpol is sending some agent of theirs, her name's Leslie something, and she'll meet you at the scene in half an hour. The school's director is still pretty upset about this whole thing, so do your best not to piss the guy off." That was Harvey's idea of a dismissal, and Frank turned toward the door and stopped.

"Can I ask why you assigned this to me?"

"You can ask anything you want. Doesn't mean I'm going to answer," Harvey said before turning his attention to his computer screen, beginning to swear under his breath. Frank made a hasty retreat. Everyone knew to get the hell out when Harvey tried to do anything with computers. E-mail alone was a challenge, and more than one keyboard had been thrown through his doorway.

Frank grabbed his keys off his desk along with the file and headed out of the office building, driving through the heavy downtown traffic to the lakeshore. He pulled into the conservatory parking lot and got out of his blue sedan that just screamed "Federal Agent." Walking around toward the front door, he saw what had to be a student carrying a violin and bow, and said, "I'm looking for Mr. Temple."

"He's in his office." She pointed the way with the bow and then hurried up the stairs. Frank couldn't help looking around the room before walking in the direction she'd pointed and knocking quietly on a closed door.

"Mr. Temple," Frank said when the door opened, "I'm Agent Frank Jennings from the FBI. We've been called in to help investigate the theft of your windows."

"Thank God," the man responded, and he opened the door fully, indicating for Frank to come into the office. "I've been frantic for two days, and I'm wondering when we'll get our windows back." Mr. Temple motioned Frank to a chair and sat in the one opposite.

"That's what I'm here to help with. Can you answer a few questions for me?"

"Of course. Anything to help get them returned. They were the source of inspiration for many of our students, and it seems wrong for them to be gone," Mr. Temple said, and Frank could see he seemed genuinely upset.

"Do you have pictures of the windows? The ones in the file I received weren't very clear. And I was wondering when you saw the windows last."

"They were still in place Monday night, and when I came in Tuesday morning, they were gone," he answered easily, and Frank continued to watch him for any hint of deception, but saw none.

"Are there lights on that side of the building?" Frank pulled out a pad and began taking notes. Mr. Temple got out of his chair, and Frank noticed that he was a strikingly handsome man, even if he was somewhat older than Frank usually liked. *Keep your attention on the case,* Frank reminded himself as he stood up as well, but he couldn't help noticing the trim cut of Temple's suit and his large, bright eyes. Blinking a few times, Frank cleared the lascivious thoughts and got his mind back on work.

"There are," Temple added a little sheepishly, leading him out of the office and down a hallway before opening what looked like a closet door. "When we did the renovations to the building, we had lights installed on that side of the building to illuminate the windows in the evening." Mr. Temple pointed to a timer mounted near the electrical box. "The lights come on when it gets dark and go off at 11:00 p.m., when we close the building." He looked dejected. "To think if we wouldn't have tried to cut costs on the lighting, we might still have our windows." Frank wanted to reassure him, but he couldn't, at least not yet, so he stayed quiet and kept his eyes open.

"Mr. Temple, there's someone asking for you at the front door," a young man said from behind them.

"Thank you, Jimmy. Tell them we'll be right out."

"That could be the person I'm supposed to meet. My supervisor said a woman was going to meet me here." Frank wasn't sure how much he should tell Mr. Temple about who he was meeting, so he kept quiet and followed Mr. Temple back down the hallway and toward the front door.

Frank saw a tall man standing near the front door, and since this wasn't who he was waiting for, he figured he'd go around the building before Leslie arrived. He was about to head outside when the man stopped him. "Are you Frank Jennings?" he asked in a pronounced British accent with a half smile, and when Frank nodded, the man continued, "I'm Leslie Carlton. I believe you're expecting me."

Frank stared. When Harvey had said Leslie, Frank had expected a woman, and Harvey obviously had as well, but instead, Frank was looking into the deepest blue eyes of the most amazingly attractive man he'd seen in a long time. Remembering where he was and what he should be doing, Frank extended his hand. "Sorry. I'm Frank Jennings, and this is Mr. Temple, the director of the conservatory." Leslie shook both their hands.

"If it's okay, we'd like to have a look 'round," Leslie said.

"Of course," Mr. Temple said before giving Frank a confused look and then walking back toward his office.

"I take it I'm not what you were expecting," Leslie stated as they walked around the outside of the building, as though he knew exactly what Frank had been thinking.

"No, I guess not," Frank answered honestly as he nervously rubbed the back of his neck with his hand.

"Happens sometimes," Leslie said, but he added nothing more.

"What's your interest in this, anyway?" Frank asked after some extended silence. "Isn't this a bit off from your usual area?"

"Yes and no," Leslie answered as they reached the area outside below where the windows had been. "I heard about the theft on the telly when I was attending a class in forensic analysis in Chicago and thought this might be related to a case I've been working on for years."

Leslie looked up at the building and then down at the ground. Frank did the same, but wasn't sure what they were going to see. The theft had been two days earlier, and the local police officers had been all through this area already.

"I could always send you the reports. You didn't need to come all this way," Frank said a little more tersely than he intended, but Leslie didn't seem to be paying any attention. Frank figured the last thing he needed was some Brit on his tail the entire time he was trying to work.

"That may not help," Leslie finally answered before kneeling down in the grass. "Looks like at least two men, maybe three," Leslie said as he stood up, wiping the dirt off his hands. "See those indentations in the grass?" Leslie said, pointing at marks Frank could barely see. "That's where they placed one of the stepladders, and here's where they placed the other. Probably strung a plank between them, and that's what they stood on to remove the windows. Lucky thing they didn't fall apart, which probably means they knew how to handle the windows." Leslie looked back up toward the vacant space where the windows had been.

"How do you know?" Frank asked.

"Hundred-year-old windows like that will fall apart if they aren't handled with a lot of care, and since there aren't bits of glass all over the turf, it's a good guess they got the windows down in one piece. Probably had frames made so they could carry them." Without further comment, Leslie walked toward the parking lot. "Probably parked about here," Leslie added, looking back toward the building, and Frank felt a bit like the newbie he was as he trailed behind the other man like some sort of puppy dog. "With the lights behind here off, and the tree here, this area would be dark and perfect for loading the windows."

"How do you know all this?" Frank finally got up the courage to ask. He wasn't particularly interested in showing his own inexperience with things like this.

"I've been working cat burglar and art-theft cases for close to ten years. I've seen all kinds of thefts, some definitely more clever than others. This one took some logistical prowess, but as long as they had cover, the street traffic masked any noise they made. Shall we have a look inside to see what that can tell us?" Frank nodded, and they walked back toward the front door of the music school. "Don't take this the wrong way, but I'm surprised they don't have a more senior man on a case like this."

Frank's hackles raised, and then he looked at Leslie's face and saw no malice, only curiosity. "I guess you usually handle bigger things than this. Sorry you're stuck with me," Frank added sarcastically.

Leslie stopped walking. "Don't get your bollocks in a wad, I wasn't being disparaging."

Frank didn't know what the hell Leslie was saying. "Let's go inside." Frank wanted to get this over with as soon as possible. Leslie could look at whatever he wanted, and then Frank could get to work hunting down the people who'd taken the windows, and Leslie could get back on a plane to jolly old England. Frank led the way into the building and up the stairs to the landing. The opening where the windows had been had glass on the inside, and Frank could see where the leaded windows had once been, as well as where the outer protective layer of glass had been. "It looks like they took the outer glass as well as the leaded windows," Frank commented, and Leslie gave him a quizzical look.

"What makes you say that?" Leslie asked.

"Because, as you said, there was no broken glass outside. They must have taken off both the outer glass and the windows themselves, along with part of the casing. There's an alarm in the building, and the police report said that Mr. Temple deactivated the alarm normally that morning."

Leslie nodded and continued looking at the window casing. "Good thinking. They were careful and knew what in bloody hell they were doing, that's for sure."

"I'd say so. They left no prints, and other than the windows being gone and the indentations in the grass that you saw, it looks like they left no other indication that they were here."

"True," Leslie said as he stood back up. "But that alone tells us something. These people were professionals. They had been here to look over the building at least once, and probably more than that. My guess is that they were even inside the building at one point. Then they would have seen the way the windows were mounted and realized that taking them out from the outside was easier than from the inside."

"The police checked out the students," Frank offered. "Wait a minute, if they were inside, they could have attended some kind of performance." Frank hurried down the stairs and along the hallway to Mr. Temple's office, knocking quickly before entering. "Have you had any performances lately?"

"Yes. We have recitals quite regularly," Mr. Temple answered, standing up to open a file drawer. He searched for a few moments and then handed Frank a few pamphlets. "These are the programs from the recitals we've held in the last six months."

"Can I keep these for now?" Frank wasn't sure what good they would do, but in his gut, he felt like he was onto something.

"Of course," Mr. Temple said, and Frank thanked him and retraced his steps, finding Leslie standing in the entry area of the building.

"I don't think we're going to find much more up there," he said, indicating where the windows had been. "Would it be okay if I catch a ride with you back to your office?"

"Of course," Frank answered, and he led the way to his car, unlocking the doors. Once they were both inside, Frank started the engine and made his way back through traffic to the office. In the lobby, he helped Leslie procure a visitor's badge, and they rode in the "lift," as Leslie called it, to his floor.

Leslie followed him to Harvey's office, and Frank made introductions before providing a verbal report of what they'd found.

"Can we speak privately?" Leslie asked Harvey, and Frank stepped out of the office, closing the door behind him. Walking to his desk, Frank watched Leslie and Harvey talking inside the office. Frank knew what they were talking about, and once they were done, Frank expected that Leslie would have requested—how had he put it?—a more senior man on this case. Placing the programs in the file with the other materials, Frank settled in his chair and began typing his notes into a report to add to the file. But as he worked, he found his attention drawn to the glass walls of Harvey's office. Frank had seen how attractive Leslie was, but he'd had his mind on the case. Now, watching him as he spoke, what he saw was mostly from the back, but what a back it was. Even in the suit he was wearing, Frank could see the man's broad shoulders. At one point, Leslie slipped off his coat, and Frank got a glimpse of a nice butt encased in suit pants.

"What's got you so captivated?" Martinson asked as he stopped by Frank's desk. "Who's the guy with Harvey?" Frank breathed a sigh of relief that Martinson thought he was just curious as opposed to lusting over the other man. The bureau itself was tolerant, but the other guys were a completely different matter. Frank had heard enough derogatory remarks over the year he'd been in the office to know to keep his personal life to himself and not let on that he was interested in guys. He wouldn't lie outright, but he wasn't going to volunteer anything, either.

"Leslie Carlton, he's with Interpol." Frank did not elaborate on his suspicions about what they were talking about. He'd get the news soon enough, and Martinson would probably stop by to rub it in again. Besides, while he might be attracted to the guy, and Leslie pushed all Frank's buttons, that didn't mean Leslie was even interested, or that Frank would actually be seeing him again after today. Frank continued watching Leslie, and eventually Martinson went on his way. Frank found he was fascinated with the way Leslie's body moved, gracefully, like the way he thought a dancer or gymnast might move. When he saw Harvey's attention shift outside the windows of his office, Frank lowered his eyes, pulled himself out of his momentary daydream, and got back to his report.

"Jennings," Harvey bellowed over the noise in the room, and while Frank didn't look, he knew every head in the room had just shifted to look at him. And he knew they were wondering what he'd done now. One mistake, and you were branded a screw-up for life. Well, maybe not, but there were times it felt that way. Frank stood up, grabbed the case file off his desk, and walked to Harvey's office, where he was ushered inside and the door closed behind him. This time Frank was motioned toward a chair, and he sat opposite Leslie while Harvey sat at his desk. "It seems we may have more than just a simple theft here, and Leslie has asked and I've agreed...."

Here it comes, Frank thought. Leslie had thought him inexperienced and green and had asked to work with someone else, not that he could blame the guy.

"Frank, are you listening?" Harvey said, and he realized both men were looking directly at him. "Like I said, Leslie has asked to be a part of your case, and I've agreed to let him work with you for the duration. He has a number of insights that will be invaluable in returning the stolen windows to their rightful owners." Harvey's expression softened a little, and Frank wondered why. "Leslie tells me that you have some interesting insights about the case."

"Well, yes. I think the thieves had to have scoped out the inside as well as the outside of the building." Frank opened the case file and pulled out the programs. "These are the recitals they've held over the last six months, and I think those would be a great place to start. If I was a thief and I wanted to scope out a place like that without being noticed, I'd blend into a crowd. And what would be better than a recital for getting into the building largely unnoticed?" Frank felt pretty proud of himself. Leslie might have figured out what had happened, at least in part, but Frank at least had an idea for going forward.

"How does this help us?" Leslie asked levelly, and Frank turned to look at him, seeing him nod slightly.

"Well, if you've ever been to a recital," Frank began—he'd been to plenty of his sister's when they were kids—"every father takes a video of the performance for posterity. I thought I'd ask the director for some of the parents who habitually make videos, and maybe we might see something unusual. If we do, we can run it through facial recognition and see if we get a hit. I know it's a bit of a longshot...." Frank wasn't sure it would pan out, but it was the only idea he could come up with. There was remarkably little evidence to go on, and much of it had been compromised by the local police and normal operation of the school, at least as far as the actual crime scene went, but that was to be expected after a few days.

"Go ahead and get on it. I'll let Leslie, here, fill you in on the other aspects of the case," Harvey explained, and Frank took that as a dismissal. Standing up, he opened the office door and stepped outside, with Leslie right behind him.

"So, where to?" Leslie asked with a pleased smile on his face.

Frank didn't know what that meant, but he did his best to keep his attention on the case, as opposed to the way Leslie's smile sent a fluttery feeling through his gut. "Back to the conservatory. I hope Mr. Temple can give us a few leads on where to start with recital videos."

"I hope so. It would be a real cock-up if we had to run down the parents of every student," Leslie said in his heavy accent. It made everything Leslie said sound sexy as hell. Frank reminded himself that he had no idea if Leslie liked guys, and he certainly had no intention of ever getting involved with anyone he worked with, even marginally. After making their way back to the elevators, they rode down to the parking level and got into Frank's car, then headed back out in traffic.

Thankfully, Mr. Temple was able to give them the names of a number of "videophile" parents, along with their addresses. Frank and Leslie spent much of the rest of the morning and afternoon running all over town, and by the end of the day, they had almost a dozen different tapes of various recitals. One of the parents had taken video at almost every one, while most had taken only some of them. "There has to be a solid week's worth of video here," Frank said as they headed back toward the office in the early evening. "This is going to take longer than I thought."

"Do we have to watch all this at the office?" Leslie asked, and Frank saw him yawn.

"No. I have a good player at my place," Frank offered. "We could get some dinner and go there. I don't have the enhancement capabilities that we have at the office, but if we see something, we can note it and look at it in more depth here at the office tomorrow. Where are you staying while you're in town?"

"I hadn't arranged for a hotel. I wasn't expecting to be here until I saw the spot on the telly. I was supposed to go back to London after the conference tomorrow, but this could be the break I've been looking for. Could we pick up my bag at the train station? I'll arrange for a hotel."

"You can stay at my place, if you like," Frank offered. He knew he was probably going to regret it, but the man was already tired, and they still had work to do.

"I don't want to be a bother," Leslie said, though Frank was already guiding the car toward the train station. Out in front, Frank pulled up to the curb, and Leslie walked into the station, returning a few minutes later pulling a wheeled suitcase behind him. Frank popped the trunk, and Leslie put the bag inside.

"How did you get them to hold the bag for you?" In the post-9/11 world, luggage without an owner was usually treated as though it carried a bomb.

"I asked the attendant at the counter and showed him my badge. I think he took pity on me because of my accent and let me put the bag in his office. I'm surprised you don't have lockers at the stations like we do in Europe," Leslie said once he'd gotten back in the car. Frank shrugged, not really wanting to explain the post-terrorist overreactions that the entire country had gone through for the last decade.

"So why don't you tell me what you think is going on," Frank said as he put the car in gear.

"Over the past ten years," Leslie began, "there have been a number of thefts of Tiffany windows, mostly from mausoleums in New York, but some in London, Paris, and elsewhere in Europe. On the surface, they don't seem related, and the thefts themselves probably aren't. Except that more often than not, when we do catch the thieves, we find that the goods are already out of the country and have been sold."

"I suppose that's to be expected—it's harder to trace the goods internationally," Frank supplied, and Leslie nodded.

"But one name keeps coming up again and again: Koshigawa. Most of the trails of these stolen windows lead to him in some roundabout way. The problem is that Japan has property laws that he hides behind. We call it the two-year rule. In Japan, if you purchased property and you've had it for two years, and it turns out to be stolen, you get to keep it regardless. Koshigawa hides behind this rule, and has amassed a huge collection of art, including Tiffany windows. The bastard has a house built of glass outside Osaka so he can display them. He calls it his museum. I've personally tracked more than a dozen windows stolen from collections in Europe back to him, but each and every time, the Japanese authorities claim the two-year rule, and we can't get near him." Leslie got more and more excited as he talked. "Last year, I investigated the theft of a huge, three-meter-tall waterfall window that came out of a family collection in Vienna. I tracked it as far as an antique dealer outside Paris who has a history of selling suspect items. I missed recovering the window by less than a week." Frustration filled Leslie's voice.

"Let me guess—he'd shipped it to Japan," Frank said.

"Exactly. The address turned out to be a front company that received the shipment and then promptly closed up shop and completely disappeared. There has been nothing since, and how much do you want to bet that in a little more than a year, it will show up in someone's collection, probably Koshigawa's, and there'll be bollocks we can do about it."

Frank navigated the streets through the northern Milwaukee suburb where he lived and let Leslie continue talking.

"I've never heard of him actually contracting a specific theft. He's usually just a buyer," Leslie continued, "but I have no doubt that he would love to get his hands on the windows that were stolen. A triptych of windows that are intact and have never been on the market could be too much for him to resist. It's like the Holy Grail to him." Leslie shifted in the passenger seat. "I want this bastard bad. He's a thief just as much as the people who steal the windows in the first place, because he and those like him help provide the market that drives this type of theft."

Frank pulled up in front of his house and parked his car, turning off the engine. "Then we need to catch the thieves before the windows can be sold and shipped out of the country, because as you said, once they leave, they're beyond us to recover." Frank got out of the car and walked around to the trunk. After pulling out Leslie's suitcase, he lifted out the box of videotapes and DVDs before closing the trunk and leading Leslie up the walk to his small house.

"This is really nice," Leslie commented once they were inside. Frank opened the windows throughout the house to let the lake breeze flow through. Then he led Leslie upstairs and showed him the guest room.

"You can stay here until you decide what you want to do," Frank suggested, and Leslie set his suitcase on the floor near the foot of the bed before following Frank back downstairs. Frank grabbed the box of videos off the hallway table as he led them into the media room. "I can order a pizza, if you like," Frank offered.

"That would be good. Thank you," Leslie replied, and Frank picked up the phone, pressing the speed dial for the local delivery.

"Is there anything you especially like?" Frank asked as he heard the pizza place answer, and Leslie shook his head. Frank placed his usual order but made it a large, and hung up. "They'll be here in half an hour. Would you like a beer?" Frank opened the refrigerator door and pulled out two bottles of Samuel Adams, carrying them to where Leslie was sitting on the sofa. When he handed the bottle to him, Leslie took it and stared back at Frank like he'd broken some sort of protocol. "If you don't want a beer, I have something else," Frank offered, wondering what he'd done to offend him.

"No. I apologize, I forgot you Yanks serve your beer practically frozen." Leslie set the bottle on a coaster. "I'll let it come up to temperature."

Frank had no idea what to say or do. "I have one that's in the case," Frank offered.

"This is fine, thank you," Leslie said, but Frank could tell it wasn't fine, so he went and retrieved one of the bottles from the basement and gave that one to Leslie. That was obviously much better, because the smile he got this time bordered on radiant. "Perfect." Leslie opened the bottle, and Frank put the first video in the player and grabbed the remote. "We need to pay attention to the crowds and try to ignore the actual performers," Leslie explained, and Frank swallowed the smartass reply that threatened to bubble up as he took his place on the sofa. "But you probably already knew that, didn't you, mate?"

Frank sipped his beer as cover and nodded as the video began to play. It took him about five minutes before he muted the volume, and both men looked at each other and laughed. "If they were truly casing the place during one of these recitals, they've already been punished enough," Frank quipped, and Leslie laughed a deep rich laugh that Frank found incredibly attractive, and he could not help watching him out of the corner of his eye before returning his attention to the screen. Most of the video was centered on the performers during the performance, but afterward, this one continued rolling as their daughter joined them, and even out through the building to the outside. The two men continued talking, and Frank mentioned they should have that portion of the video copied out and enhanced. After making a note, he ejected the disk, placing it in the case, and put another one in the player. "Rather than trying to memorize faces, let's note crowd-type scenes that we can review tomorrow."

"Good idea. You might see if they could remove the scenes and string them together. That way we could see if any faces jump out at us," Leslie suggested.

The video began, and Frank saw another performance, keeping the volume muted. He was already starting to think this was a futile effort. This video was only the performance and showed no one else. By the time the video ended, the doorbell rang, and Frank walked to the door, paid for the delivery and returned to the media room.

Leslie had made himself comfortable, and Frank nearly tripped when he entered the room. Leslie's legs were spread enticingly, his jacket and tie neatly laid over the back of a chair, his collar loosened, shirt clinging seductively to his chest. Leslie's long, shining, auburn hair, which must have been gathered and hidden in the collar of his jacket, now flowed loosely and hung below his shoulders like long strands of silk. Frank prided himself on having good powers of observation and he wondered just how he'd missed that. The man looked like sex on wheels, and the casual look on his face made Frank think that he had no idea how attractive he appeared. Frank only hoped that the effect Leslie was having on him wasn't noticeable. Regaining his balance, Frank set the pizza on the table. "Would you like another beer? I have plenty."

"Thanks, mate." Leslie tipped the bottle to his mouth, and Frank watched his throat, stifling a groan as Leslie finished the beer and then handed him the bottle. For a few seconds, Frank thought he might have been enticing him on purpose, but that had to be his imagination. Taking the bottle, Frank hurried out of the room, breathing deeply as he tried to clear his mind of the filthy thoughts that kept moving front and center whenever he got a good look at the stunning Brit.

Frank took his time getting another round, standing in the cool basement, hoping the temperatures would cool off his libido, which seemed to be running a little rampant. While he was out of Leslie's sight, Frank adjusted his pants to make things more comfortable, grabbed a beer for Leslie, and climbed the stairs. On his way through, he grabbed another beer for himself from the fridge.

The video had ended, and Leslie was removing the disk. "This one had nothing," he explained as he put the next disk in the player. Frank had to force himself to look away from where Leslie knelt in front of the television, pants clinging to a perfect rear end and what looked like strong thighs, straining the legs of his pants. He had to get hold of himself. Leslie had given him no indication that he was interested, and Frank was not about to find out the hard way. Leslie was a colleague, at least for now, and Frank was not particularly willing to be rejected or to get involved with someone he worked with, even if he had an indication Leslie might be so inclined. Frank could not allow that to happen. Rumors of his orientation would spread through the office faster than the news of him and his team raiding the wrong house.

Frank waited for Leslie to finish with the video before he handed him the beer and then turned away before sitting on the sofa and concentrating on the movie. Reaching for the pizza box, Frank stopped when he realized his lust-infused mind had completely forgotten the plates. Jumping up, he went and grabbed two from the cupboard, handing a plate to Leslie without really looking at him, and took his seat once again before reaching for his slice.

Hour after mind-numbing hour, they watched home video after home video. They'd gotten a number of crowd scenes, in addition to multitudes of hours of performance after performance. "I don't think I can take much more of this," Leslie said with a yawn. "My body's still a bit on London time."

"Thankfully, there's only one more. Go on upstairs, and I'll check this one out before coming up myself." Frank checked the clock on the player and realized it was well after midnight. He put in the last video and started it, feeling the sofa cushions shift as Leslie got up. Frank tried to force himself not to look, but the temptation was too great. Frank shifted his eyes upward as Leslie stretched his arms over his head, and he caught a glimpse of pale skin just above the handsome man's belt. Frank stared as long as he dared, looking back to the television as Leslie's arms lowered and he sat back on the sofa without saying a word. As they watched, Leslie began to shift slightly on the sofa. Frank looked over and saw Leslie's eyes drift closed as Leslie tilted toward him. Leslie caught himself and sat back upright, but not before Frank felt his warmth and the slight touch of his arm.

Frank forced himself to watch the video and keep his mind off the man sitting next to him. This infatuation was ridiculous. Yes, Leslie was attractive, and yes, he seemed to press all Frank's buttons from a physical perspective, but Frank had already had enough of the type of relationship where he relied strictly on how someone looked. He'd learned that lesson big-time already, and didn't really want to remember the details. Watching the video, he fast-forwarded through the actual performance and looked over the people behind the person doing the speaking, but didn't see anything out of the ordinary, and no one did something as obvious as trying to hide their face. Marking that portion of the video, Frank packed up all the videos, making sure to segregate the ones with pictures of the crowd before standing up. "Come on, Les, let's go on up to bed."

"Leslie, my name's Leslie," he corrected haughtily, and Frank stopped himself from rolling his eyes.

"Okay, *Les*, let's go." Frank wasn't going to rise to the bait, but he couldn't resist the temptation to push it a little, either, and he saw Leslie roll his eyes, but he didn't correct him a second time. Instead, he stood up, stretching and yawning again as Frank threw away the remains of dinner and began turning out the lights before they headed up the stairs.

Frank let Leslie use the bathroom first, waiting until he heard the door open and footsteps pad across the small hallway before opening his door. In the bathroom, it looked as though a toiletries bomb had gone off. The towels Leslie had used had been thrown on the floor, and his things sat everywhere around the sink. "What—you think I'm the maid who's supposed to clean up after you?" Frank muttered, and he began picking things up, shoving Leslie's stuff into his kit and placing it on the shelf over the sink. He picked up the towels and hung them up before getting cleaned up himself and heading back to his room, muttering under his breath.

As he stepped across the hall, he saw Leslie's door open and a startled expression from his guest. "Oh, I was about to shower before bed." Frank saw Leslie look toward the bathroom and color. "Sorry about the mess. I forgot some things, and I didn't realize you were using the same bathroom." Leslie seemed genuinely contrite, and Frank felt his anger melt away, replaced by the thrill of seeing Leslie wearing nothing but a towel.

"No problem. Do you need me to get you up in the morning?"

"If you wouldn't mind," Leslie replied. "Just knock me up when you get up." Leslie walked into the bathroom and closed the door as Frank gaped after him, wondering if he'd heard him right. Figuring it must be a British saying, Frank walked into his bedroom, shaking his head, and closed the door. Pulling back the covers, he dropped the towel and turned off the light before climbing into bed.

Feeling dead tired, Frank figured he'd go right to sleep, but he heard the water running and knew what Leslie was doing. Frank's eyes closed, and in his mind he saw Leslie standing in the hallway not two feet from him, wearing nothing but a towel. The thing that had surprised Frank was how pale Leslie's skin was, and yet in the few glances he'd seen, Frank couldn't see a blemish on the alabaster expanse. And the way his towel had clung to Leslie's small hips.... Frank kept his eyes clamped closed as if that would somehow make the images go away. He was not going to lust after a man he couldn't have, or shouldn't touch, no matter what. Frank tried to will himself to sleep, but that didn't work, not when certain parts of his anatomy definitely had other ideas. Rolling over, Frank closed his eyes and did his best to ignore the images of Leslie and go to sleep. He had many things he needed to get done tomorrow, and he needed to be awake and on top of his game, but he was not going to be able to do that if he spent the entire night thinking about Leslie—handsome, frustrating, probably straight Leslie.

*C*HAPTER 2

LESLIE heard the knock on the door and tried to figure out where he was. The bed felt strangely hard and uncomfortable, and to top it off, cold air had been blowing on him all night long, until he managed to close a vent over his bed. Yes, now he remembered; Frank had invited him to stay at his home while they worked together. Sitting up, Leslie stretched the crick out of his back and slowly stood up, his right leg giving him its usual bit of trouble. Anyone who said working the art-theft division was safe from harm was full of shite. Slowly Leslie stood up and stretched his aching leg before starting to get dressed.

A low voice came through the door. "Are you awake? I have coffee made, if you'd like it."

"Thank you," Leslie responded blearily and continued dressing. Frank sounded awake already, and after checking his watch, Leslie wondered how that was possible. They'd only gone to bed six hours earlier. Leslie knew he wasn't particularly old, but this morning he felt ancient. Lifting his case, Leslie placed it on the bed and pulled out something appropriate to wear. He'd been expecting to attend a conference and hadn't brought a lot of proper work clothes, so he made do with clean casual slacks and a shirt that didn't have too many wrinkles. Once dressed, Leslie opened his door to a quiet hallway and walked into the bathroom.

The room was spotless, as it had been the night before, and this time as he washed up, Leslie was very careful to return things to their proper place. The house was fastidiously tidy, and Leslie didn't want to be a poor houseguest. Once he'd finished, Leslie walked back to the bedroom, made the bed, and began putting his things away as footsteps sounded on the stairs. "The drawers are empty in the dresser," Frank said from the doorway. "You don't have to live out of the suitcase if you don't want to." Frank was carrying two mugs and handed one to him. "I hope you like coffee," Frank said, and Leslie nodded, sipping the dark, bitter brew.

He hated coffee, actually, and much preferred tea at any time of day, but he didn't want to appear ungrateful. "Thank you," Leslie said, looking at the wooden piece of furniture. "I didn't know how long I was to stay and didn't want to take liberties."

"I have no idea how long this will take, but it would be a shame to spend time in a hotel when you don't have to. I hate them myself. When I worked at the Milwaukee Police Department, the stakeouts in seedy motels spoiled the experience for me. You're welcome to stay as long as you like." A strange tone that Leslie couldn't understand through the adorable American accent crept into Frank's voice, and Leslie tried to figure out if he was being sincere, though he couldn't see a reason why he wouldn't be.

"I appreciate it," Leslie answered, taking another sip of the strong coffee. While he hated the taste, after drinking it for a while, he didn't feel nearly as logy, and after a few more sips, he was almost downright chipper. "God, this is strong," Leslie said with the best smile he could muster.

"FBI coffee," Frank responded, as though it explained everything.

"Am I dressed okay for the office? I only have the one suit with me and I wore it yesterday. Wasn't expecting to be dragged into an assignment, you know."

Frank took longer than was probably necessary to answer, and Leslie thought Frank might be looking him over a little more closely than was needed. "You look fine," he answered, a little too levelly, and Leslie stopped the grin that threatened. He'd sort of figured that Frank swung his way, and he'd had the notion confirmed when his host had nearly tripped over his own feet carrying the pizza box the night before.

Leslie had had to keep himself from laughing. He knew he was handsome in a certain way, and his long hair had always been eye-catching, and when Leslie was younger, quite a magnet at the clubs. But those days were behind him. Now he lived for the job and traveled all the time. Leslie was quite sure Frank hadn't figured out that he thought the sexy American appeared to be the cat's meow, and he was bound and determined to keep it that way. He'd almost lost it outside the bathroom when Frank had appeared in only a towel. Rich, tanned skin, thick arms, and a powerful chest with large, brown, perky nipples had almost done Leslie in, but he'd just managed to keep from looking for too long. Thankfully, the stiffening he'd felt coming on had waited to appear until he'd made it to the bathroom.

"When do we need to leave?" Leslie asked and then set the mug down, making sure his hair was properly tied in place before turning back to Frank.

"Whenever you're ready. I'll put the videos in the car and meet you out front."

"I should just be a minute," Leslie said, gathering his things and making sure he was ready before picking up the mug and making a stop in the bathroom to dump the rest of the coffee before stiffly walking down the stairs. After he'd placed the mug in the sink, his leg finally began to loosen up as he left the house and walked to Frank's car, and after his host locked the doors, they made their way back to the downtown office.

After riding the lift up, Leslie watched Frank wind his way through the desks. "Hey, Martinson, I've got something that needs your expertise," Frank said as he placed the box on the desk of a tall, thin man with glasses.

The man looked up slowly from his computer screen and peered into the box. "What's all this?"

"First, let me introduce Leslie Carlton from Interpol. We're working together on this Tiffany window theft. We went through all these last night," Frank said, and he pulled out the disks that held the scenes that included the audience. "I made notes of where the audience was included in the video and I was wondering if you could stream those sections together." Frank turned to Leslie. "Karl here is a master at anything electronic."

Karl took the disks, and excitement shone in the man's eyes. "This shouldn't take very long. What are you looking for?"

"We're not really sure, but we'll know when we see it," Frank said with a smile.

"Okay. Give me an hour or so." Karl returned to his screen and began placing the disks into his computer, and before they walked away, he was already typing frantically at his keyboard. Frank led them to a desk and pulled up another chair for Leslie.

"I've been thinking," Leslie began. "There is another angle we can try. If they stole the windows, they need to be able to sell them."

Frank smiled and leaned back in his chair. "I've been thinking about that too, and two things come to mind. Either they already have a buyer, and if that's true, the windows are probably already gone. But if they don't, they probably figure they'll need to hold them for a while until the heat's off. These guys don't appear to be amateurs."

Leslie nodded. "They probably aren't, but there's another option. There are people who are obsessed with these windows. Koshigawa's one of them. I know of a man in New York who used to steal the Tiffany windows out of mausoleums simply because he felt the urge to possess them. He would steal them and hold them for years before letting them go."

"That's not normal," Frank answered, but Leslie saw him sit up and lean forward.

"Neither is erecting a temporary scaffolding so you can remove windows from the outside of a building twelve feet off the ground. I could tell you stories of the things people have done to get at a work of art, and it isn't always for money. Obsession plays a big part."

Frank started his computer. "I need to update the report of what we did yesterday. I'll show them to you before I pass them on to Harvey."

He'd expected Frank to be secretive about things, but it looked as though they could work together fairly openly. After their dicey start yesterday, he'd had his doubts. "Thanks, I need to ring my office and apprise them of my status."

"Karl will let us know when he has something, so take your time." Frank turned his attention to the screen, and Leslie fished his phone out of his pocket and wandered into an unused conference room, dialing his supervisor and sharing the details of what he'd found and suspected.

"Are they cooperating?" Inspector Halley asked.

"Yes," Leslie answered. "The chap I'm working with seems thorough, if a little new, but he's smart and has good ideas. I don't know if we'll get to the windows in time or not."

"I know you want Koshigawa badly, but don't take any chances, and check in every few days. If this doesn't bear fruit, we'll bring you back. There's plenty of work here."

Leslie agreed and closed the call. There was more work than they could handle—there always was—and Leslie knew he was being given latitude because of the potential to bring down a real pain in their backside. A knock on the door caught his attention, and Leslie saw Frank waiting for him.

"Karl says he has the film edited together, and Harvey wants to see us." Frank seemed nervous, and Leslie shoved the phone in his pocket and followed him to the same office they had been in the day before.

"Any progress?" Harvey asked Frank almost before he was inside the office.

"Some," Frank answered and reported what they'd done so far. "Karl has the editing done, and we were just about to go through it."

Leslie stared as Harvey shoved a newspaper into his hand and looked over as Frank received one too. "Damned fools," Harvey muttered, and Leslie looked at the section he'd been handed. "They printed that three weeks ago in the Arts section." Leslie scanned the article and looked at Frank, who was shaking his head. "The fools decided to do an article on all the Tiffany windows in the city, and they gave the thieves a freaking roadmap to the ones stolen as well as a fucking list of every other window in town. I'll have agents contact every location and make sure they have extra security, but we need to find these guys fast before another window is stolen and we look like complete fools," Harvey said and waved his hand in dismissal. Leslie left the office with Frank, wondering how Frank could put up with someone so boorish.

"Is he always like that?" Leslie asked once they were out of earshot.

"Most of the time, yeah. Why? What's your boss like?" Frank asked him.

"Much more gentlemanly than that. Sputtering and blustering isn't going to get the job done any faster." Leslie had worked with Americans before, and he'd sometimes encountered Harvey's kind of attitude. He'd thought it might have been unique before, but it looked like it wasn't.

"Tell me about it. But most of that was for show. Just ignore it. He did help us, though, if the article turns out to be the source of the information that we need. Now we know to concentrate on only the most recent recitals. It could be a coincidence, though."

"I don't believe in coincidence. I think we'd better get started to see if we can find anything at all. This may turn out to be bloody useless, but it's all we have to go on right now." Leslie let Frank show him through the office to where Karl had set up a large television.

"I put them together chronologically," Karl explained as he started the video.

"Let's start with the last three weeks," Leslie said, and Karl looked at him questioningly. "We have reason to believe a newspaper article may have prompted the theft." The video fast-forwarded as Frank pulled up chairs for them to watch. When Karl found what he was looking for, he slowed the picture down and let it play.

"What are the blank spots?" Leslie asked as the video started.

"I went ahead and blanked out the actual people who were being taped. It wasn't likely they are the ones you're after, so by removing them I thought it would be easier to find anything you were looking for. I also blanked out the children. That way you can concentrate on anyone in the background," Karl explained.

"Good thinking," Leslie said, surprised and very pleased as he watched the faces of people. "Is there anyone who looks like they don't belong?" Leslie asked, and no one answered as they watched the faces of people sometimes far in the background. "Are those the windows?"

Karl stopped the video and enlarged the area Leslie indicated. "It appears so, yes," Frank answered, and Leslie nodded before Karl started the video again.

"That guy there," Leslie said, pointing, and Karl stopped the play. "Go back a few frames, now a few more... there. He looks like he's avoiding the camera."

"It does," Karl agreed and snapped an image from the screen. "I'll run it through facial recognition and see if we get a hit." They continued going through the videos, noting a few more people before the end.

"It doesn't seem too promising," Leslie said. "It was a good idea, though. What we really need is something to compare the faces to, and there's no guarantee that the thieves were even there, let alone allowed themselves to appear in any of the videos." Leslie looked at Frank and saw that he had the same suspicions.

"Should I continue?" Karl asked.

"Of course," Frank answered. "It's the only lead we have, and we need to run them all down."

"Okay, then let me get to work," Karl said, getting up and taking the laptop with him. "I'll let you know when I have anything." Karl left the room, and Leslie sat staring across the table at Frank.

"If we don't find anything in the next day or so, we'll have to assume the trail's gone cold, and I'll get out of your hair and make arrangements to head back to London." Leslie expected Frank to smile at that bit of news, but he seemed disappointed.

"We'll find something; we have to," Frank said softly, looking like he was deep in thought. Of course; Frank was disappointed about the case. "I keep thinking there's something we're missing, but I can't put my finger on it." Leslie nodded and stayed quiet for a while, but Frank said nothing more.

"What happened on your last case?" Leslie asked, expecting a blow-up of some sort.

"Didn't Harvey tell you?" Frank asked accusingly.

"Of course not." Leslie couldn't imagine speaking about someone behind their back like that. "I just heard some ribbing-type comments as we were walking through the office."

Frank sighed softly, and Leslie thought he wasn't going to tell him. Not that he'd blame him. Leslie knew everyone made mistakes—he had, after all. "We were assisting local law enforcement with what we thought was going to be a large drug bust." Frank's voice remained bland and neutral. "We were given an address, and unfortunately it turned out to be one house off. One of our agents was shot and injured because the suspects were tipped off, and while no one is really blaming me directly, they've been ribbing me for days. Harvey said I screwed up and should have double-checked the address, and maybe I should have. I'm not new to law enforcement, and I should have known better."

"Bollocks!" Leslie said before he could stop himself. "Were you in charge of the operation?"

"For the bureau, yeah," Frank answered and turned away, clearly not pleased with himself, before getting up and walking toward the door. "Don't want to talk about this, okay?"

"Fine," Leslie replied, "but everyone makes mistakes, though you really didn't. The person who made the mistake was the doofus who gave you the address in the first place. You took the information down correctly?" Leslie saw Frank nod slightly. "Then don't worry about it. Harvey's probably using this as an object lesson for you and the rest of the team. You just happened to be the object of the lesson." Leslie felt like the older agent giving advice to the younger man. He'd done that often enough, but for some reason that was not how he wanted to feel in this situation. The strangest urge came over him to comfort Frank, an urge that he needed to suppress. Yes, he knew that Frank was attracted to him; he had little doubt about that. And if Leslie were honest with himself, he was attracted to Frank. The man seemed smart and wanted to be tough, but Leslie could see the vulnerability inside. Or maybe for some reason, Frank had allowed him to see the vulnerability, which Leslie thought was probably a bit extraordinary.

"When I started with Interpol, I was sent on my first investigation. My partner at the time, Thorsten, and I were working to recover a set of etchings that had been stolen from a small museum outside of Munich. As we were about to raid the flat where we believed the thieves resided, I tripped and fell into the door. Thorsten had knocked, and I found myself lying on my face in the flat as Thorsten is yelling for everyone to get back and get on the floor, and I'm trying to pull myself up from the floor, my nose bleeding all over the place. Thorsten held the thieves at bay while I crawled to my feet and managed to somehow keep out of the way and not mess anything else up." Leslie noticed the tension in Frank's shoulders lessen a little. "To this day, Thorsten calls me Trip whenever I see him, and probably always will." Leslie smiled when he heard Frank chuckle, and then Frank stopped himself, as though it were the wrong thing to do. "Would it be all right to look through the case file?" Leslie asked.

Frank shrugged. "There's nothing there, but I'll go get it."

Leslie waited and used the time to try to clear his mind of the unexpected reactions to Frank. The man was attractive; there was no doubt about that. But Leslie had seen more than his fair share of handsome men, and he'd probably had more than his fair share over the years, to one degree or another. What made him pause was the way he seemed to be reacting to Frank, and it scared him a little, because feeling what he thought he might be feeling for a coworker was not good. And besides, once this case was over in a few days, he'd be returning home. So this infatuation—that's what it was, an infatuation—with Frank was simply something he'd have to put aside.

The file slid across the table, and Leslie stopped it with his hand, looking up. His eyes caught Frank's, and what he saw there startled him a bit, because in an unguarded moment, Leslie saw his own feelings reflected in Frank's eyes, and then the moment was gone. Leslie broke the contact and opened the file, needing something to cover for the fact that his mouth was dry and his stomach fluttering like he had a schoolgirl crush, except those usually didn't come with a raging hard-on that showed no signs of abating. As casually as he could, Leslie shifted in his chair and opened the file. He needed something to look at, because his eyes kept wandering to where Frank stood across the table from him, glaring.

"I didn't miss anything."

"I didn't think you had," Leslie said levelly. "But you said there was something you felt as though you were missing, and I thought we could talk things over. Sometimes it helps." *Man, the chap is touchy.* Frank warily walked around the table and sat next to Leslie.

"One of the things that bothered me was that the remaining interior glass had no residue on it at all. Not from gloves or even smudges of fingerprints that had been wiped, and it would be hard not to leave something," Frank commented as Leslie continued reading.

"They probably cleaned the window. These were definitely people who'd done this before, or had a very vivid imagination."

"Crime shows on television," Frank said, and Leslie narrowed his eyes curiously. "With all the investigative shows, like *CSI* and *NCIS*, it could be that our perps are real planners." Frank turned the page, and they continued reading. Nothing stood out to Leslie, and he closed the file, trying not to feel the slight heat from Frank's body next to him or the fact that the room felt as though it were ten degrees warmer than it actually was. He actually had the urge to reach out and touch the other man's hand, just to see what he'd feel like. He seemed to feel his hand moving closer to Frank's.

"I have something," Karl said from the doorway, and Leslie jumped slightly, thankful for the distraction. "I'm not sure it's very much," Karl added as he brought in the laptop and began rolling the video footage. "Most of the people were what you would expect, parents and family—I was able to match them to enrollees at the school. But I have a few people for you to check out," Karl said, and he stopped the video. "I can't find any information on him other than a name, John Brunner, and address from DMV." Karl moved the video forward. "The same with this guy, a David Andritch. I also have an address for him. There was a woman in the back at one point, and she seemed to be staying out of the camera, so I ran the picture I was able to get of her, as well. She's the mother of one of the students."

"Good thinking," Leslie complimented him, and he saw Frank nodding. "More than once I've arrested a woman. Once for stealing a Rubens."

"Then there was this guy," Karl explained as he brought up a still photograph of part of a man's face. "I saw him ducking behind other people in one of the shots. I don't know if he was your man or not, but the camera only glimpsed him, and he did appear to be trying to avoid it. Unfortunately, there isn't enough for recognition, but I did my best to enhance the picture."

"It's not much," Leslie said, "but it's more than we had."

"Can I get photographs of all of them as well as the addresses?" Frank asked. "We'll check them out." Karl handed him a file that contained what he'd asked for.

"I also e-mailed the information to Frank." Karl turned to him. "If you give me your e-mail address, I'll send them to you too."

"Good. I'll have all of them run through the Interpol databases as well to see if anything shows up," Leslie offered as he fished a card out of his wallet and handed it to Karl. "You did good work. Thank you."

"Yes. Thanks," Frank added with a smile, and Karl left the room with a bit of a spring in his step. "Do you want to send the photos on before we leave?"

"Sure," Leslie said, and Frank led him to a computer he could use. Leslie logged into his e-mail and sent the photos to a colleague, who got back to him almost immediately with a note that he'd send any results to Leslie's smart phone. Leslie closed the connection to their secure server and found Frank talking with one of the other agents before joining him, and together they made their way to Frank's car.

It took them a while to track down the two men, trying first at home and then following them to where they worked. David worked as an auto mechanic, and he claimed to be a family friend of one of the girls at the recital, which was easily verified. Frank thanked David for his cooperation, and they moved on to Mr. Brunner.

"I just got information from our databases, and we have nothing on either man. Our facial recognition didn't turn up anything," Leslie said as they rode in the car. The follow-up of Mr. Brunner turned up nothing as well. He was a family friend and had been dragged to the recital of his good friend's daughter.

"This is getting us nowhere," Frank said in frustration as he pounded the steering wheel with his hand. "We've wasted the day, and the thieves have gotten farther away from us. What am I supposed to tell Harvey or the director of the conservatory? I hate it when I hit a dead end."

"We all do, but it comes with the territory," Leslie replied. "Other than the guy we can't identify, we have nothing to go on. My people are still trying to see if they can get anything, but if we can't find anything, tomorrow I'll make arrangements to fly home. There's nothing more I can do here."

"So that's it?" Frank asked. "I hate it when people get away with hurting others." He thought for a while. "Let's arrange for the officers who did the original investigation to come into the office. Maybe they have something that didn't make it into the report."

"It won't hurt to speak with them," Leslie agreed, although he wasn't sure it was going to do much good. And he was right. They spent the rest of the day speaking with the officers and running down a few last details before stopping for the evening. Frank's superior didn't seem very happy, but in the end he realized they had nothing to go on.

"Hey, guys," Karl said as he met them at the elevator. "I tried enhancing the picture of our unidentified guy, but the picture just pixelated beyond belief and I couldn't get anything."

"My people couldn't either," Leslie admitted.

"You were a big help, though, Karl," Frank added as he pushed the button to call the elevator. "We're sort of stumped for now, and I'm sure Harvey will have other cases for me tomorrow. It looks like Leslie will probably be going home soon." Frank sounded a bit disappointed, and for some reason that pleased Leslie just a little bit.

The elevator arrived, and all three of them rode down together, with Karl saying good night, and Frank and Leslie walking to Frank's car. He was all out of ideas, and it appeared that Frank was as well. They remained quiet the entire drive back to Frank's. Leslie found himself looking over at Frank, and he saw that Frank kept looking back at him. After parking in front of the house, Frank got out of the car, and Leslie followed as they walked inside in silence. Leslie sat in Frank's living room, not knowing what else to do as Frank puttered but accomplished nothing. Leslie heard Frank talk on the phone for a while, and then he came in, looking a little happier than Leslie had seen him. "That was Stevens. He's home from the hospital and doing pretty well. He says he'll be able to come back to work in a few weeks."

"I take it he's the officer who was shot?"

"Yeah," Frank answered softly.

"I'm glad he's going to be okay," Leslie said.

"Me too," Frank agreed, but then he didn't seem to know where to look. Leslie squirmed slightly on the sofa as an uncomfortable quiet settled over them. "Is Chinese okay for dinner?" Frank finally asked, and Leslie agreed. Frank couldn't leave the room fast enough, and

Leslie began to let himself be happy he was going home soon. The tension between them was getting to be too much, and Leslie knew the source of it, but it appeared that neither of them was actually willing to do anything about it. Frank made another phone call, and Leslie, not willing to just sit and do nothing, went upstairs to the room he'd been using and retrieved the book he'd been trying to work his way through and brought it back downstairs. If Frank was going to ignore him, then Leslie would do something to keep his mind occupied.

Frank joined him after a while, sitting in the chair across from him. Leslie tried to pretend Frank wasn't there, but every one of his senses was acutely aware of the man's presence and every move he made. He also knew whenever Frank stole a glance at him. After trying to read the same page four times, Leslie gave up on the book and set it on the table as the doorbell sounded and Frank went to get the food. Leslie followed and paid the deliveryman for the takeaway, since Frank had paid the night before, and they took the food into the kitchen and sat across from each other. A few times it looked to Leslie as though Frank was about to say something, but he always stopped himself. Leslie wanted to talk to Frank and ask him if he was feeling the same unsettledness that he was, but his basic reserved nature precluded him from bringing it up, so they sat staring across the table at one another. Once they were done eating, Frank cleared away the packaging, and they walked back into the lounge, where Frank turned on the television.

Leslie sat down as well and stared at the telly without really paying attention. After a few hours, Leslie said good night to Frank and went upstairs. After cleaning up, he packed his bags to make sure everything was ready for the morning before climbing under the covers.

Leslie stared at the ceiling of Frank's guest room, completely wide awake. He heard Frank's footsteps, and then the bathroom door closed. Water ran for a while, and then Leslie heard the bathroom door open once again. Leslie found himself wondering what Frank was wearing and contemplated cracking his door to see if he could get a glimpse of Frank's chest like he had the night before. For a second, Leslie thought he heard Frank's footsteps get closer to his door, but they seemed to back away, and soon Leslie heard what had to be Frank's bedroom door clicking closed.

It was very likely that tomorrow would be his last day here, and provided he could get a seat on the flight to London, he'd probably be gone by the end of the day. It was unlikely he'd see Frank again. Lying in the dark room, Leslie continued staring up into the darkness and thinking. Closing his eyes didn't work, because whenever he did, Leslie kept seeing Frank wearing nothing but a towel. Getting out of bed, Leslie opened his door and peered out into the dark, quiet hallway. Looking toward Frank's door, Leslie saw it was closed, with no light shining from under it. Good sense told him to turn around and go back to his room, but the urges inside him drove Leslie toward the door, and he stood staring at it. Holding his breath, Leslie knocked softly.

From inside the room, he heard an incoherent rumble that sounded like, "What," and Leslie cracked the door. There was a clicking sound inside the room, and Leslie saw a soft light switch on. Frank rolled over toward him and began to sit up, the sheet pooling away from his naked torso. "Is something wrong?" Frank asked, and Leslie stepped closer to the bed, locking eyes with Frank.

"No," Leslie answered, his legs now rooted to the spot as Frank pushed back the covers and Leslie saw him in nothing but a pair of small briefs. Leslie stared at acres of tanned skin over planes of strong muscle. "I'm…," Leslie stammered, not quite sure what to do, although his body sure as hell was sending him a message loud and clear, and he knew it was visible to Frank, as well, through his silk boxers. Frank didn't move, and Leslie hoped he hadn't read everything completely wrong. But from the way Frank's gaze bored into him, Leslie knew he hadn't, and he took a small step forward, reaching for Frank and just touching his chest with his fingers. "If the answer is no, say so now," Leslie whispered, and then he swallowed hard when Frank moved closer and Leslie felt warm hands on his skin.

"You look like alabaster, do you know that?" Frank asked as he moved closer, their chests touching. "A perfect alabaster god, and you're right here in my bedroom." Frank tilted his head and kissed him, not lightly and sweetly, but as though Leslie were being possessed by a much larger predator. "You were playing with me yesterday, weren't you? You knew I thought you were attractive."

Leslie nodded. "I was hoping," he answered, and then Frank kissed him again, pulling their bodies together roughly and with enough force that Leslie grunted softly as the air left his lungs. And then he was being kissed again as Frank's skin rubbed lightly against his. Damn, the man was hot, and every time he touched him, Leslie's body felt as though it were on fire. He tried to take control of the kiss from Frank, but the other man was not allowing it in any way. Leslie felt Frank press his body against him, moving him back and closer to the bed, holding him around the waist while stroking a hand through his long hair.

"I've wanted to feel this since I saw you take it down yesterday. I thought you were attractive before then, but with your long hair, you look amazingly sexy." Frank stopped talking and kissed him again, hard and possessively, like he was never going to let Leslie go. And for tonight, Leslie hoped he didn't. By the time Frank pulled his lips away, sucking Leslie's lower lip along with it, Leslie strained for breath and felt himself being pressed back onto the bed. Then he was falling and bouncing on the mattress as Frank stepped back and pushed away his briefs. Leslie gasped out loud, his eyes widening as Frank stood in front of him in all his masculine, naked glory. Frank reached for the waistband of Leslie's boxers, and they were yanked off his legs.

"I take it you don't believe in taking your time," Leslie said between panting breaths.

"Time is the one thing we don't have," Frank answered as he climbed onto the bed, prowling like a cat, with Leslie as his prey. Leslie shivered when Frank skimmed his hands over his thighs and then up his hips before sliding over Leslie's stomach and chest. "You must work out," Frank said before placing his lips against the skin on Leslie's stomach, and Leslie felt a flutter run through his muscles when Frank licked a long, searing line to his left nipple.

"So do you," Leslie managed to say as Frank's lips continued doing incredible things over his skin before returning to his lips. The intensity of Frank's kisses increased, and Leslie felt Frank's warm skin pressing to his as Frank's weight settled on him. Almost instinctively, Leslie opened himself to Frank. He'd rarely done that with any of his longer-term lovers, let alone someone he'd just met, but Frank seemed to command it, and Leslie couldn't stop himself. He knew instinctively that not only would Frank never hurt him, but his deep eyes told him that Frank would always put his partner's pleasure over his own.

Frank's gaze seared a path through Leslie, right into his brain. "Fuck, you're amazing," Frank told him softly, and Leslie didn't know what to say in return, not that he could when Frank took his lips once again. Then Frank tilted his head, lips locking around Leslie's nipple. A lick, a nibble, a bite, Frank tortured his chest in the most exquisite way, and all Leslie could do was squirm, thrusting his hips forward as Frank drove him wild. "Everyone who sees you for a week without your shirt on is going to know what I did to you and how I made you feel."

Leslie loved the idea that long after he'd felt it, he'd have a reminder of Frank with him, even if it would only be temporary. Arching his chest forward, Leslie ached for more, whining when Frank didn't quite provide enough sensation and grunting when it seemed as though he couldn't take any more. "Frank." Leslie knew he was begging, but it didn't matter.

"You'll get what you need," Frank explained, his voice rough and deep. "But when I'm ready to give it to you. I'm gonna build the excitement and keep you on the edge until you scream for me to let you come. I want your eyes to cross and the air to rush from your lungs, and I want you to remember me for as long as you live." To accentuate his point, Frank wrapped his fingers around Leslie's cock, holding him tightly without moving his hand. Leslie's legs throbbed along with his cock, and he tried to thrust his hips, the need for just a little more almost overpowering. "I know what I'm doing," Frank whispered.

"Fuck," Leslie whined softly, panting harder when Frank's thumb made a single swipe around the throbbingly sensitive head of his cock. "You're going to kill me."

Frank stilled, gripping tighter. "No, I'm not. I'm going to make you feel alive." Suddenly, all sensation was gone, and Leslie blinked a few times, wondering what had happened. Frank moved off the bed, standing next to it. Leslie was about to ask what was going on when he was twisted, his legs dangling over the side of the bed. When Leslie reached instinctively for his aching cock, Frank lightly batted his hand away. "Touching you is what I get to do."

Leslie gripped the bedding and waited, his cock bobbing against his stomach. When Frank gripped him again, Leslie sighed, but when Frank spread his legs, kneeling between them, and took the head of his cock into his mouth, Leslie cried out and tried to press deeper into the moist heat, but Frank held his hips still. "Is this what you want?" Frank asked softly, sliding his lips further down Leslie's long shaft.

"Yes," Leslie answered roughly.

"Okay, but you can't come," Frank admonished, his eyes meeting Leslie's, backing up his words. Leslie nodded his understanding and moaned uncontrollably as Frank took him deep.

"Holy hell!" Leslie gasped, and Frank sucked him hard, driving Leslie out of his mind with the quick bobbing of his head. Gripping the bedding, Leslie had to will himself not to come after about ten seconds. His legs shook, and his hips tried to thrust forward on their own. Leslie's vision narrowed, and his brain screamed for release, any kind of release, from the overwhelming waves of sensation. Then, just as quickly as he began, Frank let him slide from his lips, and Leslie lifted his head and saw Frank grinning back at him like the cat who'd eaten the canary. Leslie tried to speak, but found the power to say anything coherent had left him when Frank nearly sucked his brains out through his dick.

"Lift your legs, Les," Frank said, and Leslie pulled his still shaking thighs toward his chest, gripping his hands behind his knees. Leslie expected to feel fingers against his opening and braced himself for the slight burn of the initial breach, but instead he felt Frank's hands on his butt, tugging his cheeks apart, and then the hottest wetness he'd ever felt in his life skewered him open. Leslie felt his vision begin to swim. Frank did things to his backside with tongue, lips, and fingers that Leslie never thought humanly possible. Small nibbles alternated with deep probing thrusts of what had to be the most incredible tongue on the planet. Leslie had had guys rim him before, but nothing like the way he was now being devoured completely. Moans echoed and bounced off the bedroom walls, building and compounding in Leslie's ears. He barely registered that he was making those sounds until Frank stopped.

"Damn, you're vocal," Frank said deeply before blowing warm air onto his hot, wet skin.

"I can't help it," Leslie said somehow—the first words he'd been able to form.

"I know, that's what makes it so fucking hot," Frank told him before working a finger into his body.

Leslie felt Frank curl his finger and then touch the spot inside him before retreating again, only to be replaced by the touch of Frank's searing tongue. Leslie lost track of the number of times Frank alternated between lips, tongue, and finger. His mind had long stopped processing the passage of time or anything else that was happening to him other than Frank's touch. One finger became two, and still Frank continued to somehow keep him just this side of coming. Leslie's body was being played in a way he'd never felt before.

Frank slipped his fingers from Leslie's body, and Leslie waited. He felt the bed shift, and opening his eyes, Leslie saw Frank straddle him, Frank's long, thick cock sliding up his chest. Leslie reached for it, but Frank held his arms down. Opening his mouth, Leslie felt Frank's cock slide between his lips and into his mouth.

Leslie sucked hard and as deep as he dared, bobbing his head as Frank's incredibly rich, masculine flavor burst onto his tongue. Leslie felt Frank move his hips slowly, guiding the large cock in and out of his mouth. Frank felt wonderful and looked even better, his powerful body towering over him. Reaching around Frank's body, forgetting Frank's admonishment, Leslie grabbed Frank's butt, using that touch to help control the speed of his thrusts. Leslie saw Frank lean back and then felt Frank's hand around his shaft, stroking as Frank continued thrusting lightly. "Damn you look so good," Frank told him, and Leslie sucked harder and deeper as a thank-you. Leslie felt Frank's body tighten, and then Frank stopped his hip movements. Frank's cock slid away from his lips, and Frank lowered himself to the bed, kissing him hard. "You're amazing, you know that?"

He'd been told many things over the years, but Leslie had never been described as amazing before. But he didn't argue, and after another hard kiss, Frank slithered down his body until he was standing on the floor once more. Leslie saw Frank reach to the table, and he watched as Frank retrieved a packet and a small bottle. Enraptured, Leslie watched as Frank stretched a condom over his thickness before lubing both it and him. Then Frank leaned forward. "Lift your legs again for me," Frank said, and Leslie readily complied, feeling the head of Frank's cock touch his opening. "I'm going to fuck you until you forget your own name," Frank growled, and then he pressed into his body, stretching his opening with that thick cock.

The air shot from Leslie's lungs as Frank slid deeper and deeper, a steady pace that barely gave him time to adjust before giving him more and more. "God, Frank!" Leslie cried, and he almost begged him to stop, but Frank pressed deeper, nearly overloading Leslie's brain with wave upon wave of sensations that overflowed, one on top of the other.

Frank tugged his body forward, and Leslie scooted on the bed, Frank buried deep inside him, hips tight against his ass. Then and only then did Frank give him a chance to breathe. But the respite was brief, and then Frank pulled out with agonizing slowness, only to drive back into his body with a deep, forceful grunt as the bed jumped slightly across the floor. To say Frank fucked like a madman was an understatement. How long Frank drove into him Leslie had no idea. All he could remember were the sensations and his head rolling back and forth on the mattress as his entire consciousness narrowed to Frank. The large man towered over him, powerful chest thrust forward, stomach crossed with deep lines that undulated as Frank moved his hips back and forth. Sweat rolled down his skin, making him glisten in the low light, almost like he'd been oiled. Speech had long given way to incoherent grunts and moans that filled the room and spoke more eloquently about what each of them was feeling than any poem or sonnet ever written.

Gasping for breath, Leslie lifted his head and caught Frank's eyes in a silent plea for release. Frank's only reply was to wrap his fingers around Leslie's length and stroke him in time to his deep, mind-shattering thrusts. Leslie had no idea how long he was going to last, and then delicious pressure built deep inside his stomach and Leslie felt his balls tighten. There was no going back now—Frank had brought him past the point of no return, and Leslie arched his back, mouth opening wide in a silent scream as he released all the pent-up longing and desire that Frank had generated in him.

Through his post-orgasmic haze that seemed to go on and on, Leslie floated, and once he came back to some sort of awareness, he heard Frank crying out his own release. Leslie barely felt anything, but Frank jumping and throbbing inside his body cut through the cobwebs. Still trying to catch his breath, Leslie tugged Frank to him, holding the incredible man close as they both caught their breath.

Leslie gasped and squirmed when Frank slipped from his body, but neither of them made any effort to move for quite a while. Finally, Leslie felt Frank lift his weight and then leave the room, returning a minute later with a warm cloth that glided over Leslie's hot skin. Reaching up, Leslie ran a hand through his hair and was surprised to find it soaked with sweat.

After cleaning him up, Frank tugged Leslie to his feet and helped him through the house to the bathroom. His legs felt so unsteady, Leslie welcomed the help, yet managed to stand as Frank turned on the water and then helped him under the spray. "I'm sorry," Leslie said, feeling like a bit of a child.

Frank chuckled softly. "Do you have any idea how sexy you look right now? How hot? Knowing that I'm the one you allowed to let you feel this way is completely amazing. You certainly have nothing to feel sorry for, unless you regret what happened." A tinge of worry seeped into Frank's voice.

"No, I don't regret it at all. I don't know if I'll be back, but you gave me an experience that I'll measure everyone else by for the rest of my life," Leslie said as he felt Frank step behind him, arms around his waist, holding Leslie to his strong body. The water cascaded over both of them, and for a while neither moved. Eventually Frank reached for the shampoo, and Leslie felt his fingers washing his hair. Leslie let his head rest back against Frank's chest, enjoying the soft, light touches.

"Rinse your hair, and I'll wash your back for you," Frank said softly, and Leslie stepped under the spray, closing his eyes as the water washed away the lather. When he stepped forward, it was Frank who smoothed his hair out of his eyes before grabbing a bar of soap. "Stand still," Frank said, and Leslie stopped moving and let Frank's hands wander all over his skin. The gentle, caring touch soothed away the excitement, replacing it with a deep warmth that Leslie hoped would never fade, but knew would only last until he stepped on the plane. Then the feelings would fade and be replaced with the everyday and the life he was going back to. Pushing those thoughts out of his mind, he let himself concentrate on the feel of Frank's hands. Earlier they'd been demanding and exciting; now they soothed and caressed. The difference was striking and extremely sensual.

Frank didn't ask him to return the favor, in regard to the washing, and before Leslie could offer, Frank had turned off the water. He stepped out of the shower and wrapped Leslie in a bath sheet. "Are you feeling more like yourself?"

"Yes. Actually I feel pretty amazing," Leslie said softly, "but my hair is going to take hours to dry." He didn't want to complain, and he said it as lightly as he could, but it was true. Frank chuckled softly and opened a drawer, handing him a hair dryer before leaving the bathroom. Leslie chuckled before plugging it in and carefully blowing his hair dry. Once he was done, he wrapped a towel around his waist and stepped out of the room. He was trying to decide if he should just return to his room when he heard Frank softly call his name. Leslie walked toward the room. When he saw Frank lying on his side, naked, Leslie dropped the towel and walked toward the bed.

CHAPTER 3

"WHAT'S with you the last few weeks?" Karl asked as he passed Frank's desk. "You haven't said anything remotely derogatory to me in nearly two weeks. I'm starting to think you don't love me anymore." Karl chuckled as he continued walking toward the door.

"Did you ever find out anything on our mystery man?" Frank taunted, and Karl stopped walking for a second.

"Did you?" Karl asked, his eyebrows lifting slightly before he turned his head and walking toward the door.

Frank turned back to his paperwork before getting up and hurrying after him. "Karl," Frank called as the elevator doors opened. He caught up to Karl just as he was about to get inside. "Would you like to get a drink?" Frank knew that Karl was gay, and after the way he'd been feeling for the last few weeks, Frank needed to speak with someone. He might give Karl a hard time, but Frank thought Karl could be trusted with his secret.

"I don't think I'm your type, big guy," Karl quipped, but he didn't get into the elevator. "What is this, 'gay FBI agents' night out'?" Karl's expression hardened slightly, the smile slipping away. "You serious?"

"Sure," Frank answered, his stomach a little jumpy, but he needed to talk to someone.

"Okay. I'll meet you at the Pink Triangle in half an hour." Karl pressed the call button again, and when the door opened, he stepped inside, and Frank returned to his desk, getting his things in order. Half an hour later, he stood outside the bar in Milwaukee's gay neighborhood for a minute before going inside. Frank had been to places like this more than once, but he'd never been here, and as soon as he stepped inside, he knew why Karl had picked it. Frank hadn't pegged Karl as gay for a very long time, probably the geek thing, but this place seemed to be the man's nirvana. In addition to pictures of men, the walls also had numerous patrons' high scores on various video games, and instead of a pool table, there were video games in the back of the bar. On top of it, this was the first drinking establishment Frank had ever been in that was absolutely smoke-free and actually smelled fresh.

"Hey, Frank," Karl said as he walked up next to him.

"Interesting place," Frank said as he looked around, and Karl laughed.

"We're not all big, hunky bruisers like you." Karl looked toward the bar and said, "Although you seem to be popular." Karl's laughter continued. "Come on, I have a table over here. And no, our geekiness is not contagious—you won't wake up tomorrow with the urge to play *Sim City 3*."

"Very funny," Frank retorted before shaking his head. "I actually wanted to speak with you about something rather… serious, at least to me."

"Is it about the guy from Interpol?" Karl asked, motioning Frank to a chair.

"How'd you know?" Frank asked, definitely a bit confused and concerned that he'd been wearing his emotions so close to the surface.

Karl seemed offended and leaned forward in his seat. "I may not look like you, but I am an agent just like you and I have eyes."

Frank held up his hands. "Sorry, I wasn't impugning your abilities, not in the least."

"So I take it I'm right? What happened?" Karl asked, his expression softening.

"He was staying at my place for a few days, and the last night he was here, we...." *Damn it, why is this so hard?* He'd had sex before, many times, and he'd never felt shy about talking about it. "We spent the night in the same bed," Frank confessed, using the euphemism rather than give Karl any details.

"That must have been some night," Karl commented quietly, "especially if you still can't get him out of your mind." Karl waved to the bartender, who walked over and placed two beers on the table. "Thanks, Larry," Karl said, and Frank saw their eyes link as they held each other's gaze for a longer time than necessary. Larry moved away, and Karl lifted his beer. "As I was saying, that must have been a night to remember."

Frank pulled his eyes away from Larry and returned his attention to Karl. "Let's just say the man was special, okay?"

"Then what did you want to talk about?"

Frank sighed. "I don't know. I miss him. He was something else, and I can't stop thinking about him."

"Have you called him?" Karl asked, and Frank shook his head. "Have you communicated with him at all?" Again Frank shook his head. "You're pretty pathetic."

"So are you," Frank countered lightly before leaning across the table. "Have you even noticed the way Larry looks at you or thought about the way you look at him?" That got him a sour look from Karl. "Sorry, man," Frank continued, "that's none of my business." Frank lifted his beer and noticed that Karl snuck a peek at the bartender before returning his attention to the table. "I guess I needed someone to talk with who understood how things are."

Karl narrowed his eyes. "Look, just say what you mean and drop the macho FBI agent act, okay? No one here is going to judge you, and you don't have to be tougher than everyone else because you're gay and need to prove that you're just as good as anyone in the office." Karl sighed when he was done speaking.

"What crawled up your butt?" Frank quipped, wondering if this was such a good idea in the first place.

Karl sighed. "Do you have any idea what it's like to be invisible? No one notices me until they need computer help. I'm a trained agent, and Harvey never sends me out on calls or assigns me to cases. I sit in the office all day supporting everyone else's cases, but never get one of my own." Karl gulped his beer. "It's not your fault, and I know you wanted to talk to me about the sexy Interpol agent."

"How about we make a deal? If anything breaks on this Tiffany window case, I'll get in touch, and you can come on the call with me. You worked on the case with us, so you're already familiar with it, and that way, I won't have to get another of the agents to come along. But now you have to answer my questions."

"Okay, it's a deal, and I have your answer… call him!" Karl rolled his eyes dramatically. "If you want to get him out of your head, you need to talk to him and stop being all testosterone-y about it. Who knows, he may be thinking about you too."

"But he's in London," Frank explained.

"They have these things called planes. Arrange to take your vacation there and hump like rabbits for a week, talk things through, get to know one another, whatever it is you want to do—but stop moping about it." Karl downed the rest of his beer. "And now that the talking portion of the evening is over, let's bond over a game of *Mario Cart*."

"I thought you said it wouldn't rub off," Frank teased.

"I lied," Karl stage-whispered and led them toward the back of the bar. He explained the game, and they stood in front of the game console. Cars began running, and Frank kept crashing while Karl sped around track after track ahead of everyone else. "These things give you great reflexes," Karl explained as he made a turn, his entire body flowing along with the game as though he were really in the car along with his gorilla character.

"My only question is why you're the gorilla and I'm…."

"Princess Peach," Karl explained with a laugh. "Lessons in humility. Besides, I need to get in touch with my inner gorilla, and you definitely need to talk to your feminine side." Karl zoomed past, lapping him in the game.

"I don't have a feminine side," Frank gritted through his teeth as he pressed button after button to go faster, adrenaline coursing through him as he coaxed his car forward and only ended up falling off the edge of a rock face, much to the delight of the people who were watching. Thankfully, Karl let it go and celebrated his win with a beer that Frank bought. He wasn't sure he'd gotten an answer to his questions, and yet... maybe he had, because he now realized that the answers had to come from within.

"Ready to play again?" Karl asked with a smile, but Frank handed the controller to one of the other guys and stood back as that guy and Karl dueled it out to whoops and hollers that filled the bar. More people came in as the night progressed, and the use of the video games continued even as gay boys did what gay boys do regardless of their geeky status. A few guys tried to buy Frank a drink, but he really wasn't interested. Not that there was anything wrong with the guys in the bar. They'd all been great. Over the past few weeks, Frank had found he wasn't interested in general. Not that he didn't get horny; he just wanted one particular person to be horny with.

After a while, Karl put out the word that Frank had gone through a bit of a breakup, and the offers of drinks stopped, but more of the guys invited him to play. And to Frank's surprise, he felt more of a camaraderie with these men than he ever had in a gay bar before, and it came as a bit of a pleasant shock. As the evening wore on, Frank ordered food, lots of it, and shared it around with the others before saying good night to the guys and to Karl, then leaving the bar to head home. Frank hadn't had much to drink, and felt comfortable that he was sober enough as he drove through the city streets toward his house.

Inside his comfortable house, Frank sat in the living room and turned on the television, watching the evening news before climbing the stairs to get ready for bed. He stopped himself from walking into the guest room where Leslie had stayed; that was a bit too maudlin for words, and instead took a shower and brushed his teeth before walking into his bedroom and climbing between the cool, crisp sheets.

Eventually Frank fell asleep, and he dreamed the most amazing dream, with a long-haired brunet doing the most amazing things to him with his mouth. When the brunet opened his mouth, he made a ringing sound.

IT TOOK Frank's mind a few minutes to process that the ringing was coming from outside his dream. Reaching for the nightstand, Frank cracked his eyes open as he found his phone. "Yeah?" he asked sleepily.

"Is this Jennings?" the man's voice on the other end of the line asked.

"Yes," Frank answered as he forced himself awake.

"We were told to call you. Got a call about half an hour ago about a home invasion in progress. You had put out a call that you wanted any information on the theft of Tiffany windows. We believe the perpetrators were after one of those windows."

Frank came instantly awake and began to get dressed even as he got the information from the officer over the phone. As soon as he hung up, Frank dialed Karl. "Get up, Karl. I got a call on a window." Frank gave him the address in Mequon. "Get there as soon as you can." Karl said he would, and Frank hung up. After pulling on his pants, Frank got his shoes and socks on, then grabbed his keys as he headed for the door, still buttoning his shirt as he made his way to his car.

Frank sped down the freeway, arriving at the house in question fifteen minutes after he'd been called.

"You Jennings?" a Mequon police officer who looked barely out of diapers asked as Frank approached the drive. Frank had barely stopped his car and turned off the engine before he'd grabbed gloves and was out his door. "I'm Craig Colston." They shook hands briefly.

"Yes. My partner is on the way. What do we have?" Frank asked immediately, all business.

"The homeowners surprised the burglars in their home before they could get very far. They'd disabled the alarm system and were working to remove the window from its frame when the homeowners began making noise. The thieves left the house without taking anything with them."

"Can you show me?" Frank asked as another car pulled up, with Karl getting out and joining Frank. "This is my partner, Karl," Frank explained, already walking toward the house, and after saying a quick hello, Frank heard Karl rush up behind him. "Not being rude, but I need to get in there before they mess up everything," Frank explained as he pulled a pair of gloves out of his pocket and handed another pair to Karl.

Inside the large home, Frank found officers speaking to two men, one of them holding a young girl. Frank didn't wait for an introduction. "Are you all right?" Frank asked, and all heads turned toward him. Frank reached into his pocket and pulled out his identification. "I'm Frank Jennings, and this is Karl Brody, we're with the FBI."

The two men looked at one another, and the one man began moving his hands. Both the girl and the other man did the same. To Frank's shock, Karl stepped from behind him and began making similar signs.

"I'm Brian Watson, and this is Nicolai," the man holding the girl explained. "He isn't able to hear."

Frank nodded. "Can you tell me what happened?"

Brian settled the little girl on the sofa before standing up. "Why don't you explain why you're here first? This is just a simple theft, isn't it?" Frank could see some doubt settle into the man's expression.

Frank noticed that a number of the other officers had stopped and were listening in on the conversation. "Could you give us a minute?" Frank asked. Craig nodded, and the others left the room. "You may have heard about the theft of the windows from the Conservatory of

Music downtown. I believe these incidents could be related." Frank looked to the large wall, where a window still hung in its frame. The thieves had apparently started to unbolt the frame from the wall when they'd been interrupted. "Along with the conservatory, you and others were featured in an article in the paper about Tiffany windows, and we believe that article brought you as well as the conservatory to the attention of the thieves." Frank stopped while Brian finished signing to the other man.

After a while, Brian motioned Frank toward a chair. "What would you like to know?"

"Let's start with what happened," Frank explained and took the offered seat while Karl stood. Frank saw him pull out a pad. Frank smiled his thanks, and Karl nodded in return.

"I didn't hear anything at first. Nicolai woke me up and told me that something was wrong in the house. He didn't know what, but he said he could feel something wasn't right. Then I heard a slight movement downstairs. Getting out of bed, I quietly walked to the upstairs alarm panel and hit the button to set off the alarm, but nothing happened. I went back into the bedroom and called the police. Neither Nicolai or I made a move to go downstairs, but Zoe heard the movement and left her room," Brian explained, and Frank saw Brian begin to pale.

"Thank you," Frank said and turned to the girl, who looked about twelve. "What's your name?" Frank asked gently.

"Zoe," she answered. At first Frank thought she was scared, but that didn't seem to be the case at all, because she readily began to talk. "I was getting a glass of water when I heard something downstairs. I was wondering if Dad or Nick were down there, so I began walking down the stairs and heard men whispering softly. I knew it wasn't either of them because Dad and Nick never whisper. There's no need— they sign to each other. I peered around the banister and saw two men in our living room, and they were trying to unscrew Nick's window from the wall." Zoe seemed more excited than scared, although Brian looked terrified.

"Did you see them?" Frank asked, and Zoe nodded her head.

"They looked like men you see on television, all dressed in black. They weren't wearing hats or anything, but they both had gloves on. When Dad and Nick made noise, I hurried up the stairs. I don't think they saw me, but I heard worried whispers and them moving things around. They must have been taking their tools because most of them are gone." Zoe slipped off the sofa, and Frank saw her start to reach under it.

"Don't touch anything," he said with a little more force than he meant to, and Zoe stood back up, looking hurt. "You were a big help," Frank said, softening his voice, "a really big help." Frank got down on his knees and looked beneath the sofa, where he saw a screwdriver and a few long bits of metal. They could have been drill bits, but Frank wasn't sure. "Would you like to come to my office tomorrow? I'll show you all around and show you some pictures on a computer. Maybe you can help us identify the men you saw."

Zoe nodded and smiled. "Do you have a lab like they do on *NCIS*?"

"Yes, and I'll see if our 'Abby' can show you around." He got questions like that all the time, especially from kids.

"Can you tell us what this is all about and why the FBI is involved in robberies?" Brian asked, and Nick stood up, extending his hand to Zoe and leading her out of the room and up the stairs. Frank called in the police officers and told them what was under the sofa. When Craig joined them, Frank asked for copies of their report, and they readily turned the investigation over to him, along with the evidence they'd gathered.

"I'll take charge of it," Karl said and followed the officers while Frank and Brian moved to another room.

"There's the possibility that these windows are being stolen to order, but I can't go into more detail with an open investigation. I'm hoping that the thieves who entered your home are also the ones who robbed the conservatory. They left barely a trace there, but you surprising them seems to have tripped them up. Maybe we'll get something to lead us to them." Frank looked closely at the other man, something in the back of his mind nagging at him. "Do I know you from somewhere? You seem familiar."

"I'm an attorney downtown," Brian answered, and Frank kept rifling through his memories. "I won a very high-profile art case a few years ago."

"The Woman in Blue," Frank replied. He remembered hearing about it and reading the story in the newspapers. "My God. These people couldn't have picked a worse house to rob."

"If there's anything we can do, just let us know. Nicolai and I will bring Zoe to your office in the morning." Brian walked to a table and picked up a card. "This is my office number. I can be reached there most of the day, and if I'm out, my admin knows where I am."

Frank handed Brian one of his cards as well, and then Karl returned from the other room. "I have the evidence from the police, and I swept the room, as well, to make sure there was nothing else. We'll need to get prints from you for elimination," Karl told Brian. "Please stay out of the room in case we need to check anything again," he added.

Brian nodded his assent. "Is there anything else?"

"No. Thank you for your help. We have everything for now. We'll see you in the office in the morning." Frank shook hands with Brian, and then he and Karl left the house. "It looks like we may have caught a break on this one."

"Yes, it does," Karl agreed. "Are you going to call Interpol?" Karl waggled his eyebrows, and Frank nearly protested, but stopped himself. Instead, he pulled out his phone and fished into his wallet for the number that Leslie had given him. Pressing the numbers, he waited for the call to connect.

Leslie's voice came over the line. "Hello."

"Les, it's Frank. I was wondering if you could make a trip back to Milwaukee."

"You got a break?" Leslie sounded excited.

"Another robbery, and this time they were interrupted and got careless. But you'll never guess who they tried to rob. You remember a few years ago, the big court case about *The Woman in Blue?*"

Leslie chuckled. "Yeah, I remember it. We helped bring pressure on the Austrians to do the right thing, why?"

"It's one of the lawyers who won that case. They tried to steal a Tiffany from the wall of their living room. Look, if you can get here in a few days, we may be able to find out if Koshigawa is involved. They left evidence at the scene this time, and if I were them, I'd be figuring out how to pull up stakes and get out of Dodge, so we may not have much time." Frank could feel excitement racing through him at the thought of Leslie coming back to town, but he had to keep that out of his voice.

"I'll see what I can do and get back to you," Leslie said, and Frank thought he heard a hint of the same excitement in his voice. "Talk to you soon. Cheers." The call ended, and Frank shoved his phone back into his pocket before leading Karl out of the house.

"I'll meet you back at the office," Karl said as they approached the cars. "Is he coming?" Karl asked, and Frank shrugged, not quite sure if he trusted his voice not to betray his anticipatory excitement. "Okay. I'll meet you downtown."

"You did real good, Karl," Frank complimented him before opening the door and getting into his car for the drive to the office. It didn't take long before Frank was parked near the federal building, yawning as he rode the elevator to his floor. The office was really quiet, and Frank went to his desk, turning on his work light and booting up his PC. He heard Karl come in a few minutes later, carrying a box of tagged evidence. "We need to log all that in and get it to the lab for analysis."

Karl nodded. "I'll also see if I can get a computer set up so we can put together a composite of the men. Maybe one of them will be our mystery man from earlier, and we'll be able to fill in his face and identify him."

"We can only hope," Frank answered and got to work typing up everything he knew. Once Karl had the evidence logged, they walked it to the lab and put a rush on it, especially the pieces found under the sofa. The excitement and adrenaline lasted for a few hours, until Frank could barely keep his eyes open, and even coffee didn't seem to help much. Karl, on the other hand, was a bundle of energy and never seemed to stop. By the time Harvey came in, Frank had his report ready.

"Heard you got a call last night," Harvey said as he walked through the office. "You could have called."

"Didn't need you, and I figured I could fill you in this morning," Frank told him. "I e-mailed you a preliminary report, but we got physical evidence this time."

"Who went with you on the call?"

"Karl," Frank answered, and he saw the surprised look on Harvey's face. "He did a great job. We've already got the evidence logged and down to the lab. They're working on it now." Harvey didn't say anything more, but Frank could tell he was pleased. Frank hadn't been sure how Harvey would react to him taking Karl on a call; the two of them had never really gotten along. Frank had always thought it was because Harvey was rather old school and Karl was definitely new age.

Frank was caught up, and there wasn't much more he could do until the lab finished their work. While he knew he could run down there, all he would end up doing was pestering them, and that would piss them off, so he forced himself to instead go to the locker room and lie down on one of the benches, dozing off in a matter of seconds.

"Frank," Karl said softly, and he opened his eyes, slowly sitting up. "They're here with Zoe."

"Thanks," Frank said as he stretched his arms over his head. "I'll be right out." Karl stared at him. "What?"

"Nothing," Karl answered, but didn't turn away, and then he smiled. "You know you're kind of cute when you wake up!" Karl hurried out of the room as Frank leaned toward the door, taking an air swipe at him and missing on purpose. Stretching one more time, Frank got to his feet and left the locker room.

At his desk, he greeted Brian and Nicolai, with Karl signing for both of them. "Are you ready, Zoe? Karl is going to help you draw a picture of the men. Just do your best."

"I will," she assured him, and Karl led them all to a conference room. She and Karl sat at one end of the table, behind a computer, while Frank sat with Brian and Nicolai. After retrieving cups of coffee, Frank sat quietly, waiting until they were done. Frank listened to Karl as he guided Zoe through the process of describing the man she'd seen. Frank could tell both Brian and Nicolai were nervous, and a few times they signed between themselves.

"Is this the first man?" Karl asked Zoe, and she answered, "Yes," very excitedly, bouncing in her chair. "Excellent. I'm going to send this picture to Frank, and then we can start on the second man."

"I think we can leave the two of them alone," Frank said, and Brian nodded, getting up and tapping Nicolai on the shoulder, and they all left the room. Frank led them to where they could sit down, and just then his phone rang. It was the lab, telling him that they had something for him, and he explained that he would be down as soon as he could. It took Karl another fifteen minutes before he and Zoe emerged from the conference room.

"She was amazing. Zoe remembered details I never thought possible, and we got really good composites." Karl and Zoe shared a high five.

"Can we see the lab now?"

"I called down, and they are really busy today, but they said that if you could come back after school one day this week, they will be happy to give you the entire tour from beginning to end." Frank hoped he wasn't disappointing Zoe too badly, but he had to get this case moving forward.

"I'll bring you back," Brian prompted, and Zoe nodded.

"You promise?" Zoe asked, and Frank knew she was going to hold him to it.

Frank held up his hand in a salute. "I promise." Then he held out his hand and Zoe shook it, sealing the deal.

"We need to get you to school and let Karl and Frank find the guys who broke in," Brian said before thanking both Frank and Karl, shaking their hands before. Then he led both Nicolai and Zoe from the building. Frank couldn't help watching the gentle way Brian treated Nicolai. Even though they never actually touched, it was clear just from the way they looked at each other and interacted that there was great feeling between them. He'd seen it that morning when he was at their house, and he saw it now, and that was what he wanted. Turning away from them as they reached the door, Frank hurried to the stairs and descended to the floor below, walking down the hallway to the lab.

"Frank, what took you so long?" Shelley asked as he walked through the door, barely looking up from her workstation. "Give me a second." Shelley was small and thin with gorgeous black hair and eyes the size of planets. All the male agents did their best to catch her attention, and she could always get them to do her bidding with a simple smile. Of course, that trick never worked on Frank, and maybe that was why he and Shelley had become fast friends. There was no sexual tension, and they could simply be themselves around each other as opposed to all the other silliness. Shelley continued typing as Frank looked around the room, his hands by his sides. He knew better than to touch anything—the last agent who had still had trouble typing. "I was able to get fingerprints off the screwdriver. There are multiple sets, but fortunately for you, they didn't overlay too badly, and I was able to isolate them."

"Were you able to run them?" Frank asked as excitement grew in the pit of his stomach. He loved this point in cases, when he had a lead and an answer was within his grasp.

"I'm doing it now," she answered and stopped typing before turning to look at Frank. "I can't figure out why they'd need a drill bit. That has me puzzled."

"I have a theory on that," Frank told her, and she waited impatiently. "They didn't. I bet they were planning to use one as a screwdriver and there was a bit already in the drill. They had to take it out, and once they had, they lost track of it and it rolled under the sofa." He waited to hear her thoughts, but she said nothing. "Sometimes the simplest explanations are the right ones."

"Maybe. I wasn't able to get anything off of it, though. It was clean except for bits of drywall dust. I'll call you when I get something on the prints, but it could take a while. The database is running really slow this morning for some reason, but I'll call you when I get results." She turned back to her keyboard.

"Thanks, Shelley, I really appreciate it," Frank told her and lightly fist-bumped her shoulder. Frank knew she was smiling even if he couldn't see it, and left the lab a happy man. As he was climbing the stairs, his phone rang. Pulling it out, he saw an international number, and his heart skipped a beat.

"Hey, Les, what's the good word?" he asked.

"Wish I had one. My superiors think this theft might be linked, but they won't send me over unless there's some direct link to the case I've been working on." Frank thought Leslie sounded as disappointed as Frank felt, but he did his best to keep it out of his voice. He wasn't even sure that Leslie was thinking about him the way he kept thinking about Leslie. Frank knew it was a cop-out, but he didn't want to ask in case Leslie didn't feel the same way. They might never see each other again, and Frank wanted to keep the memory of their night together untainted by what might be reality. "Please keep me informed and let me know if you find a link to Koshigawa."

"I will," Frank replied, and he looked around him to make sure no one could overhear him. The words were on the tip of Frank's tongue to tell Leslie that he couldn't seem to stop thinking about him, but he stopped. It wouldn't do either of them any good to say anything, so Frank kept quiet. It took him a second to realize that the line had gone silent.

"I should let you go. Please…," Leslie stammered for a second before his tone changed to all business. "Let me know if there's anything we can do."

Frank said he would and disconnected the call. Maybe one night was all they were meant to have together and Frank should be satisfied with that. Putting his phone back in his pocket, Frank schooled his expression and continued walking up to his desk. He'd barely sat down when Shelley called and told him she'd gotten a hit on the fingerprints. "I'm sending it to your e-mail right now."

Frank signed in and opened the file, motioning Karl over to his desk as Martin Zvolensky's picture appeared on his screen. "That's one of the men Zoe described this morning," Karl said excitedly before pushing Frank out of the way and taking over his PC. "I can do this faster." Karl swiftly moved his fingers over the keyboard, and soon both pictures displayed on his screen side by side.

"That's definitely him," Frank said. "Let's go pick him up."

"I'll get a warrant," Karl said, rushing back to his desk, and Frank walked to Harvey's office, sticking his head inside.

"We've identified a suspect. Karl and I are going to pick him up. He's getting the warrant now."

"Are you sure you want to take Karl?" Harvey asked.

"Is there a reason I shouldn't?" Frank countered.

"His field experience is almost nonexistent," Harvey answered. "He's brilliant at computer forensics, but I don't think he's suited to fieldwork." Harvey seemed to give it some thought. "I suppose we'll never really know unless we give him a chance. Watch out for him," Harvey admonished before returning to the paperwork on his desk. By the time Frank got back to his desk, Karl had the warrant, and they headed out to Mr. Zvolensky's last known address.

THE house was in one of Milwaukee's old south-side neighborhoods. Frank parked around the corner and turned to Karl. "Keep your firearm handy and let me take the lead. You have my back," Frank said, and he saw the seriousness in Karl's eyes. "If you're threatened, shoot."

"I know, Frank," Karl said.

"I know you do. But knowing and doing are very different things. Keep your eyes and ears open, and you'll be fine," Frank reassured him. He remembered his first partner on the police force telling him the exact same thing on their first call. "Always look for and expect trouble."

Frank parked the car across the street from the house, and they got out. Frank noticed that Karl looked up and down the street and all around him before approaching the house, following Frank. Frank approached the door, standing off to the side, and he had Karl do the same before knocking on the door. Frank heard no movement inside and was about to announce himself when the door opened slowly and a small man with white hair stared up at him from a wheelchair.

"Good morning, we're looking for Martin Zvolensky. Is he here? We're federal agents and we have a warrant for his arrest."

The man looked shocked and backed his chair away from the wall. Frank could almost see the older man's heart breaking as his eyes lowered. "He's upstairs in his room."

"Is he armed? Does he have a gun?" Frank asked, and the man shook his head.

"I don't believe so," he answered, and Frank drew his weapon and carefully made his way up the stairs and down the hallway. All the doors were closed, and Frank carefully peered into every one—most appeared as though they weren't being actively used. At the last door, Frank quietly turned the knob and found himself looking at a rather shocked Martin Zvolensky, who stared back at him from beneath the covers. "Martin Zvolensky, you're under arrest for burglary, grand theft, and breaking and entering. Put your hands where I can see them and don't make any fast moves."

"Can I get dressed?" he asked and slowly lifted his hands from under the covers.

"In a minute." Frank had him lie on the floor and cuffed his wrists. "Karl," Frank called and heard footsteps on the stairs, "grab a blanket off the bed so Mr. Zvolensky can cover himself." Frank turned to the naked man on the floor. "Tell Agent Martinson where to find clean pants and a shirt, and you can change into them when we get you into custody."

"In the dresser," he answered, and Karl pulled on gloves before opening drawers and retrieving some clothing. In one corner of the room was a plastic bag, and Karl emptied it and stuffed the clothing inside.

"Let's get him downtown," Frank said, and he helped Martin to his feet and got the blanket around him before leading him down the stairs. Frank had seen disappointment in parents' faces before, but the man who Frank guessed was Martin's father looked completely lost and heartbroken as they took his son out of the house. Frank guided a silent Martin Zvolensky into the back of his car and closed the door. Then he looked around and saw Karl talking to the old man for a few minutes before joining him at the car.

The ride downtown was quiet, with neither Frank nor Karl saying much. Karl kept a close eye on their suspect as he squirmed in his blanket. Arriving at their building, they pulled into the secure entrance and transferred their suspect out of the car and through the building before placing him and his clothes in a secure interview room. Only then did they remove the cuffs so he could get dressed. "We'll leave him alone for a while and let him think about what's happened before we talk to him," Frank explained. "I'll do the interview, but you can watch from the next room. I need to get ready for the interview. Would you keep an eye on him?"

"No problem," Karl answered, and Frank returned to his desk, his mind running through how he wanted to handle the interview. After gathering his materials, Frank stopped by Harvey's office and brought him up to date before going to conduct the interview.

Opening the door, Frank stepped into the room and sat across the table from Martin. "You know your rights," Frank reiterated before placing his file on the desk. Usually suspects protested their innocence or yelled for an attorney, but Martin did neither.

"What's going to happen to my dad?" he asked in a small voice. "I take care of him, and without me he can't take care of himself."

"You should have thought of that before you committed those robberies," Frank said levelly. He knew he came off as heartless, but he could not show weakness of any type. "You want to tell me what happened?" Martin stared back at him and said nothing. Frank expected him to ask for an attorney, but he didn't. "I've got your fingerprints on a screwdriver left at the scene of your endeavors last night, and we have a witness who can place you at the scene." Frank slid a copy of the composite drawing across the table and saw Martin's eyes widen, and what little fight was in him died away.

"It wasn't my idea." Martin began. "I need to take care of my dad, and his medicines cost a fortune. I was at this bar, and a guy said he needed someone to help him with a job. He said I could earn fifty grand."

"This guy have a name?" Frank asked gently, prompting Martin to keep talking.

"He said it was Douglas, but I saw papers when we were riding in the car that had the name Dale Kortevan on them. He said all we needed to do was lift some windows out of a few buildings, and that he had a buyer for them already. Said I could get fifty Gs out of it, and that would take care of Dad for a long time. I wouldn't have done nothin' like this if Dad didn't need his medicine. He's got Parkinson's and can't walk no more."

"Where did you take the windows?"

"To a storage facility near the airport on East Layton near Pennsylvania," Martin answered, and Frank got up and walked toward the door. "What's going to happen to me?"

"That's up to the courts, but I suggest you get a lawyer and consider cooperating when we catch your friend." Frank opened the door and left the room, closing the door behind him. Harvey was in the hallway, and Frank filled him in.

"Do you know the storage facility?" Harvey asked.

"Yes." Frank knew exactly the place.

"Okay. You and Karl go there and see what you can get. I'll send another team to pick up Kortevan," Harvey told them before walking back down the hall.

"I spoke with Mr. Zvolensky back at the house, and he's dependent on his son for his care. The man really seemed lost and almost petrified," Karl said.

"I know someone at Elder Care. I'll see if they can stop by and make sure he's okay," Frank said as they walked briskly toward their desks. "Get the second composite that Zoe made. We'll show it at the storage facility and see if that doesn't open some doors." Frank was so excited he could barely stand it. They were so close Frank could almost taste success, but he knew that was when things usually fell apart. Karl got the drawing, and Frank made a phone call to a friend at the senior citizen's advocacy group, explaining the situation. They promised to get someone out to Mr. Zvolensky today. Frank hung up as the elevator doors opened, and they hurried inside. The damned thing could not descend fast enough.

FRANK drove as fast as traffic would allow. "That was a nice thing you did," Karl said as Frank drove, and Frank glanced at him momentarily before returning his attention to zooming down the freeway. "You didn't have to help Mr. Zvolensky." Karl sounded a bit surprised. "You aren't nearly the unfeeling asshole everyone thinks you are."

"No, I'm not." Frank wasn't about to admit, even to Karl, that he really did care. If he let it show with every person who crossed his path, he wouldn't be able to survive. "You have to develop a thick skin in order to survive doing what we do. And yes, you're one of us, regardless of your lack of field experience. Our job is to help where we can, but you can't get emotionally involved."

"And your coping mechanism is being an asshole," Karl teased. "I always knew you were a good guy, down deep. I just never figured I'd locate a shovel big enough to find it."

"You really like poking the bear, don't you?" Frank growled, but he knew Karl wasn't going to buy it.

"I like teasing you because you need it," Karl replied and then remained quiet as Frank took the curves past I-894 nearing the airport turnoff. "Why did you ask to join me for a drink?"

Frank didn't shrug and actually tried to pretend he was too busy driving to answer the question. He really wasn't sure why he'd asked, but he knew what had prompted it. And the disappointment that he wasn't going to be able to see Les again was keeping him from discussing it. The emotion was too close to the surface, and he needed to be 100 percent focused on the task at hand.

After they pulled up to the storage facility, Frank parked outside the office and walked up to the window, flashing his badge to the young kid sitting behind the counter. Frank saw his eyes widen and caught a hint of fear in his demeanor. "We're investigating a series of thefts, and we have reason to believe that stolen merchandise is being held on the premises." Karl handed him the composite drawing, and Frank showed it to the man. "Have you seen him?"

The kid nodded. "I saw him this morning. He drove in about half an hour ago, and I haven't seen him leave, but I don't know which unit is his," the kid explained quietly.

"Check your records for the name Dale Kortevan," Frank instructed, his energy ramping up. He and Karl waited while the kid typed at what looked like a grungy keyboard.

"I don't have anything under that name," the kid answered nervously, picking up on Frank's energy.

"What's he driving?" Frank demanded.

"A blue pickup truck," the kid answered.

"Stay inside and keep down. Disable the gate, let no one in or out, and stay out of sight," Frank barked as he motioned for Karl to get back in the car as he heard the front gate rolling closed. Getting into the car, Frank started the engine and pulled away from the office, slowly driving down the first aisle. No truck, so Frank continued driving toward the back of the facility, looking down the aisles. At the second to last aisle of the large facility, Frank saw a truck parked outside the door of an open storage unit.

"I don't see any movement," Karl said, and Frank nodded, already wary and in hostile-suspect mode. He parked out of sight and got out.

"I don't either. Stay behind me and watch our backs." Frank walked toward the unit, gun in hand. As he approached the truck, he saw no movement and heard no sound from inside. Walking silently, Frank peered around the corner of the unit. The space was filled with boxes and wooden crates of various sizes. Frank continued listening as he entered the unit. He was about to turn to leave when he heard footsteps.

"Don't move a muscle," a gruff voice said, and Frank turned, feeling a gun pointed at his chest. Frank instinctively fell to the ground. A gun went off and Frank braced for pain, but felt nothing except the warm, hard concrete digging into his knees.

"Move, and I'll put a bullet in your other knee!" Karl said over the sound of cries and groans of pain. "Frank, are you okay?" Frank heard Karl ask as he heard the unmistakable sound of a gun sliding across concrete.

"Yeah," he answered, getting to his feet. Frank wished he had a camera. Karl stood over the man like Dirty Harry, face set, expression hard. All that was missing was the "go ahead, make my day.'" Frank got to his feet and cuffed the man. "Call for an ambulance."

"It's only a flesh wound, ya baby," Karl told the suspect before he called for medical assistance and backup. Frank walked around slowly, making sure he was okay before taking a look around the storage unit.

"I bet most of this stuff isn't even his," Frank taunted with a smile on his face.

"I'm not saying anything, and I want my lawyer," the suspect said between whines of pain.

Frank didn't acknowledge him and continued looking around. Sirens sounded in the distance, getting louder, and soon an ambulance as well as police cars pulled down the aisle toward them. Once police officers and EMTs had custody of the suspect, Frank called Harvey to bring him up to date and requested additional agents on the scene. The storage unit was huge, and the walls were lined with dozens of boxes and crates.

More cars arrived, along with a truck. Everything in the storage unit was tagged to be placed into evidence and carefully loaded into the truck. Frank was itching to see if the windows were in any of the flat crates, but everything had to be entered into evidence first.

The EMTs finished with the suspect, and the police officers agreed to transport him downtown for them, so Frank and Karl followed behind and supervised his placement in an interview room. They were able to confirm that his name was indeed Dale Kortevan and that he'd rented the storage facility under a false identity. But he refused to say anything without a lawyer, so they waited.

"Let's let him stew for a while. We can go down to evidence and see what we found," Frank suggested, and he could see the same curiosity he was feeling reflected in Karl's expression.

"I wanted to thank you for what you did," Frank began a little uncomfortably as they walked toward the elevator. "You had my back and did a great job." Frank turned to Karl after pressing the call button. "Was that shot a fluke?"

Karl shook his head. "No, it wasn't. Everyone takes one look at me and sees geek," Karl began as the door opened. "But I'm a crack shot, and if anyone messes with me, I can take them down with my bare hands. I may not be large or strong, but I'm fast and wiry." Karl walked into the elevator. "I'm getting a little tired of being overlooked."

Frank had a feeling that after today, there wouldn't be many people overlooking Karl anymore. If they didn't realize it, that was their problem, but Karl was a good agent, and Frank was impressed. He also realized that he trusted Karl. Frank didn't trust easily, and yet he had trusted Karl almost instinctively. Riding the elevator down, he couldn't help looking at Karl with fresh eyes.

In the evidence room, they walked into a major amount of activity, all being overseen by Shelley. "I have to perform forensic analysis on everything, so don't touch anything without gloves and don't move anything any more than necessary," she said to the group of agents placing the items in lockup.

"Have you opened any of the crates?" Frank asked her, and she smiled.

"Check over on the tables," she told him, inclining her head toward the far wall. Frank looked to where she indicated and saw three tables, each with a large wooden crate lying open on it.

"Come on," Frank said with a smile, and they walked over. Each crate contained what looked like a leaded glass window. Since it was dark, the colors were hard to discern, but the design looked like dogwoods to Frank, and he couldn't help smiling over at Karl. "We did it." Frank grinned, and Karl did the same. "Mr. Temple at the Conservatory of Music is going to be thrilled."

"So what's in all the other boxes?" Karl asked, turning back to where the unloading was finally being completed.

"We'll find out once they've had a chance to unpack everything, but for right now, I feel like celebrating. I haven't eaten a thing since last night and I'm starved," Frank said as his stomach rumbled.

"We still have a suspect upstairs," Karl reminded him, throwing water on his food plans. "I'll grab a couple of sandwiches from the machine, and we can eat fast before you question him."

"Before *we* question him," Frank corrected, and they headed for the elevator to go upstairs. Once they reached their floor, Karl headed toward the break room, and Frank went to his desk to get his materials together for the interview. After Karl returned, they ate hurriedly, shoving the food in their mouths before heading to the interview room.

"YOU can't make my client wait all day," Kortevan's lawyer said as soon as Frank and Karl walked into the room. He was obviously trying to intimidate them, but it wasn't going to work.

"I can make him wait as long as I want. He's under arrest and isn't going anywhere. He can either sit in this cushy room or I can transfer him to a cell without air-conditioning and he can sweat, literally, for a few hours." Frank pulled out the chair and sat down, looking deeply into Kortevan's dark eyes, trying to get a feel for the man. He was definitely hard, unfeeling, and had no care for anyone else he hurt. This was a man who cared only about himself and his own self-preservation. Frank knew he could use that. "I know you stole the windows from the Conservatory of Music and tried to steal another one last night from a home in Mequon. Your partner in crime has told us all about you."

"So? I don't have anything to say," Kortevan responded, and his lawyer stood up.

"I believe we're done here."

"We're not done until I say we're done. He can sit here until he rots, and you can as well. I want answers and I'm going to get them." Frank glared at the attorney. "You have access to your client and can advise him all you like, and I can question him until I'm blue in the face if I like. He's under arrest and in our custody, charged with multiple felony charges. We have plenty of evidence that even you can't dispute, including an eyewitness, fingerprints, as well as the testimony of his accomplice. And to top it off, he tried to rob the home of one of the most distinguished attorneys in the city, so we have plenty of backing." Frank turned to the suspect. "I want the answer to one question: what were you going to do with the windows?"

Frank watched as Kortevan squirmed and looked at his attorney and then up at Karl. Frank didn't follow his gaze, just stared daggers into him and waited. But he said nothing. A soft knock on the door interrupted them, and Frank looked to Karl, who stepped outside. Frank wanted to scream. He could see Kortevan beginning to waver until the interruption, and now he could almost see the defenses being rebuilt before his eyes. Karl poked his head back into the room and motioned for him. Frank got up and left the room, closing the door behind him. "What is it?"

"I have something for you," Shelley said, bouncing on the balls of her feet. "It seems your suspect is wanted in three states, and Interpol is looking for him, as well. Apparently he's wanted in a number of countries. While he may not be big-time, this guy has definitely gotten around."

Frank smiled and thanked her before walking back into the room, with Karl right behind him. "Well, well, it seems we're not the only ones who want a piece of you." Frank couldn't help smiling at the attorney. "It seems the Europeans are interested in your client, as are a number of states, including Arizona. I wonder how he'd fare in a prison in the middle of the desert." Frank slid back into his chair. "Like I said, I want to know who you were planning to sell the windows to."

Kortevan looked at Frank, and Frank knew he'd won. Kortevan was going to tell him anything he wanted to know, and Frank got his answer in one word. "Koshigawa." Frank had to stop himself from breaking into a grin.

CHAPTER 4

LESLIE had plenty of time to think as he rode in the back of the bumpy plane. He still wasn't quite sure what had happened, but he'd gotten a phone call from Frank, and suddenly things had been put into motion around him that nearly had his head whirling. Either Frank or his supervisor had some pull, because after speaking to his own supervisor, Leslie found himself hitching a ride in an extra seat on a US military plane across the Atlantic. He had gotten some information from Frank during their call, though, and it seemed that he'd been able to tie the thefts in Milwaukee to Koshigawa. He had no idea what the plan was, but he'd learn that when he arrived.

The thing that had him most curious was whatever was going on between him and Frank. Their one night together had been explosive, at least for Leslie, and he knew there had to be more than just sex involved. Leslie knew there was for him. Frank could be prickly, he'd seen that, but no one could have made love to him the way Frank had and not have it mean something. Leslie didn't think that was possible. Sure, he'd had hot sex before, but nothing had touched him as deeply as being with Frank had. Leslie had tried to get the memory of that night out of his head for over two weeks, and nothing had worked. The way Frank's eyes had met his was burned into his brain, and Leslie had tried to decipher that look over and over. He'd kept telling himself he needed to let it go, but he couldn't.

Leslie shook his head and looked around at the other passengers on the plane. Most were men in uniform, but some were families with a few children. The engines droned on, and Leslie sat in his seat, thinking. He tried to focus his mind on anything other than Frank Jennings, but it wasn't working. Noises swirled around him, and Leslie ignored them all. He knew he was acting like a schoolgirl, wondering if Frank liked him. They'd had a single night together—it wasn't as though it was a marriage proposal, or that they'd professed their undying love. They'd had sex. But Leslie could not stop himself from wondering if Frank was feeling the same thing he was. Closing his eyes, Leslie tried to put these unproductive thoughts out of his head. It took some effort, but Leslie closed his eyes and cleared his mind, trying to sleep, because as soon as he arrived, he knew he'd need to hit the ground running.

Eventually Leslie must have fallen asleep, because he woke as his ears popped, and he could feel the plane descending. After they landed in Washington, DC, Leslie followed the instructions he'd been given. Within an hour he found himself on another plane, this one actually headed for Milwaukee. During the flight, he brushed up on all the information he had on Koshigawa and the way the man operated. By the time he could feel the plane descending, Leslie was as up to date as he could be, not that he needed to go over all this information. Most of it he'd committed to memory, but it helped keep his mind off other things. Leslie put his materials away in preparation for landing and stared out the window as the ground got closer and closer.

Once they'd landed, Leslie grabbed his bag and left the plane with everyone else, descending the stairs and looking around. He wasn't sure what he'd been expecting, but he had not anticipated Frank standing on the tarmac, waiting for him with a smile on his face. "Let's get your bags, and we'll head right down to the office," Frank told him over the wind and the sound of other plane engines. Leslie grabbed his bag off the cart and followed Frank to a parked car.

Once his bags were in the trunk, Leslie got into the car, with the sounds of the airport cutting off as soon as the door closed. He waited for Frank, who got in the car a few moments later, and soon they were driving out of what looked like a military base and then onto the regular streets.

"I didn't know art crimes were a military priority," Leslie said as he looked over at Frank, who appeared intently focused on his driving.

"They aren't, but Harvey pulled some strings. We knew that time was of the essence, and you're the expert on the man we're after." They stopped at a signal, and Frank looked over at him. Leslie looked for anything of what he remembered seeing that night two weeks ago, but Frank's expression was all business. They were alone in the car, and Leslie had hoped to get some indication from Frank regarding how he felt. "We recovered the windows, but no one outside the bureau knows," Frank continued, and Leslie thought that maybe he already had his answer.

Sighing to himself, Leslie turned away from Frank to stare out the window. "What's the plan?" he asked, keeping the near-crushing disappointment out of his voice and concentrating on the job at hand, even as he could feel his stomach clench. In that moment, looking out the window, Leslie realized just how much he'd been looking forward to seeing Frank again and just how much he'd been hoping that what he'd thought he'd felt from Frank wasn't his imagination. But obviously it was, and Leslie would be the consummate professional.

"That's our first order of business," Frank answered. "We need to decide how we want to handle this opportunity. We have a meeting in a few hours to lay out options."

"Good," Leslie answered before checking the time. "Did anyone reserve a hotel for me, or should I try to find one? I'd like to check in and clean up before the meeting."

"I thought... I—" Frank began, and Leslie felt a surge of hope, but Frank stopped speaking and continued driving.

"You thought what?" Leslie prodded, turning away from the window to look at Frank, and he saw him biting his lower lip. "What were you going to say?"

"Nothing," Frank answered quickly, probably a little too quickly.

"Sure... nothing," Leslie responded before reaching around the back of his head and pulling his hair free, letting it fall to his shoulders.

It felt good loose, and Leslie saw the gleam in Frank's eyes. "What was it you were going to say?"

"I thought… I hoped… that you'd want to stay with me," Frank said, sounding like a petulant child.

"Who said I didn't?" Leslie asked testily. "From your macho attitude, I thought you weren't interested. Hell, since we left the airport, you haven't even smiled at me. What was I supposed to think?" Leslie shook his head and turned back toward the window. "I haven't been able to stop thinking about you," Leslie admitted, a little afraid of being rejected or of the attraction being one-sided, but he really needed to know where he stood. If macho Frank wanted to be professional and that was all, Leslie could deal with that, or at least he'd figure a way to deal with it.

"I've been the same way," Frank explained. "But I wasn't sure how you felt. I mean, it was only one night, and I wasn't sure if…." Frank banged his hand on the wheel lightly. "Sometimes you make me feel all goofy, like I'm in high school again, and I don't like not being in control."

"You think you're the only one?" Leslie turned to face Frank. "I wondered for two weeks if you felt the same thing I did. I got to the point that I figured it must have been my imagination. You never called, and when you finally did, you were all business. Is that a Yank thing?"

Frank scoffed lightly. "I think it's a guy thing or a 'don't talk about shit' thing. You didn't call either, if you recall."

"I know," Leslie admitted. Maybe Frank had been feeling the same doubt he had, since neither of them had been willing to simply pick up the phone and ask. "And for the record, it's not a Brit thing, either. I think it was a 'scared the best night of my life was a fluke' thing." Damn, that was hard to admit, but he had, and now Leslie waited to see how Frank reacted.

"It wasn't a fluke, and I'll definitely prove it to you," Frank told him as he turned his eyes to meet Leslie's. The look made him shiver, because the desire he'd seen two weeks earlier lay bare in Frank's eyes. "But unfortunately, first we have an art buyer to take down."

Leslie smiled. "I want this guy bad! He's been a thorn in both the legitimate art world's backside and mine for a long time."

"We'll get him. But you know there's another who'll take his place," Frank said cynically.

"Maybe. But this is also the chance to highlight to the world in a big way what Japan and countries with similar laws are doing. That's the only way we'll get them to change, and maybe if we catch him, it will help cast doubt on his entire collection, and then we might have a chance to find out just how much of it is stolen." Leslie could feel the thrill of the hunt beginning to build. That was part of what he really loved about his job. Many of his cases involved years, and sometimes decades, of searching and tracing shady transactions and deals. "There are works in his collection that we believe were stolen almost a decade ago."

Frank pulled into the lot and parked his car, then led Leslie to the building and toward a secure elevator that opened when Frank swiped his badge. They rode in silence, but Leslie could feel the excitement that seemed to dance between them. When the doors opened, Frank led him to his desk. "You remember Karl," Frank began as the other man looked up from his computer. They shook hands. "He's been a great asset on this case."

"Of course. It's good to see you again." Leslie could tell that something had happened between them. The tension he'd noticed between the two men on his previous visit was gone.

"Would you like to see what we recovered?" Karl asked proudly.

"Absolutely," Leslie answered, and the two men led him back toward a different elevator that they rode down. When the door opened, Leslie realized they were in what had to be part of the basement of the building, and he could see a number of items on shelves and tables.

"There was so much that we had to use this space to house it," Frank explained as Leslie stared at all the items.

"Is all this stolen?" Leslie asked, staring at Tiffany lamps, paintings, antiques, and God knew what else.

"We believe so. We're still trying to figure out where it all came from. Our suspect has clammed up, and I think he's holding out because he figures he can get a better deal, but we'll figure it out without him." It was obvious that the suspect had not endeared himself. Frank led him to a set of tables. "I believe this is what we're interested in." Frank turned on a light and Leslie peered into the open crate, the unmistakable shine of Tiffany glass sparkling back at him. "Makes you want to see them in the sunlight, doesn't it?" Frank asked, and Leslie nodded, speechless as he gazed at the windows.

"No one knows you've recovered all this, do they?" Leslie asked, still looking at the stunning windows.

Both Frank and Karl shook their heads. "We don't want to alert anyone just yet. Not until we decide how to proceed. I have some ideas, but I'm hoping you'll have some as well. You know our quarry better than anyone, and before we rush into this, we're hoping you'll have some insight."

"I think I do. Is it possible to get something to eat before our meeting?" Leslie looked at Frank for a second.

"You two go on," Karl said with a slight smile. "I'll make sure everything's ready in plenty of time."

They walked to the elevator and rode up, getting out at a floor that contained what appeared to be some sort of cafeteria. "We don't really have time to leave, so get something quick, and once we're done tonight, I'll see you get a proper dinner," Frank told him almost conspiratorially, and they got in line.

While they ate, Frank brought him up to date on all the details of the case. Once they were done eating, Frank led them down to the conference room, where people had already begun to gather. Leslie knew some of the people around the table from his previous visit, and he was introduced to the rest, although he probably wouldn't remember their names.

"As most of you know," Frank began after he'd closed the door, "it appears we've caught a fairly major art thief here in town, but we expect to find a still bigger fish, and there's a possible international connection. Leslie Carlton from Interpol is here, and I'm going to let him explain." Frank motioned to Karl, and all eyes turned to a screen on the wall.

"Hiro Koshigawa," Leslie began, as the man's picture from the file he'd provided to Frank before he left London filled the screen. "He's extremely wealthy and a world-class collector. His major passion seems to be windows, primarily Tiffany, but he also collects anything that catches his fancy. He's got money to burn and thinks nothing of buying items with a questionable past, and he uses the liberal Japanese property laws to his advantage." The screen changed again. "This is his home, and from all accounts it's a museum filled with Tiffany glass, jealously guarded. No law enforcement from outside Japan has ever gotten inside, not that it would do any good, because after two years, any item purchased in Japan by an 'innocent party' becomes their property. Koshigawa is not an innocent party, but up till now, no one has ever been able to prove it."

The pictures on the screen began to change, moving from window to window. "These are some of the items we believe are in his collection. Some were stolen from here in the US, and others from Europe." Pictures of a spectacular tree-of-life window flashed on the screen. "This was stolen from a cemetery outside London." The pictures changed again. "These came from a private home in New York, and these from a convent. He has no qualms about buying anything that he desires. We believe there are many other items in his collection that we don't know about."

"So what's changed?" Harvey, Frank's supervisor, asked from the head of the table.

Leslie smiled. "As far as we know, he's never contacted anyone to actually steal anything for him. He's always purchased his items on the open or gray market. But you've apprehended someone who claims to have been working to procure things directly for him. That's new and a bit frightening, because it means he's getting bolder. And it's also safe to assume that the man you apprehended isn't the only one working for him." A thought occurred to Leslie, and he turned to Frank. "Have you checked out your suspect's attorney? Do you know if Koshigawa is paying his bill?"

"He doesn't appear to be," Frank answered.

"Since our suspect has helped us," Harvey began, "we've agreed to testify in court as to his limited cooperation in this matter, but only based upon the silence of both him and his attorney. We can't be sure about the attorney. But if news of our suspect's arrest does leak, then we'll have the attorney on ethics charges so fast it'll make the weasel's head spin." Leslie couldn't help smiling at Harvey's American phrasing. *His* supervisor would be so proper. "According to the information from our suspect, he hasn't met Koshigawa personally. They communicated through a middleman, but he's not giving up the name. It would be possible for a man to pose as Kortevan and make contact with Koshigawa, but we don't know how to do that without giving ourselves away."

"I may be able to help with that," Leslie said, returning his attention to the room. "One of the reasons why we have never been able to pin anything on old Hiro is because he rarely does actual business outside Japan. But I think that a set of three windows might be enough of an enticement to get him here, if we dangle the bait right. I'm sure you have contacts who could get out the word that Kortevan is looking for a buyer for the windows, spread it around that he wants more money than Koshigawa is willing to pay. If I'm right, Koshigawa will act personally, because these windows are like the Holy Grail to him. The man is avid and obsessed when it comes to his collecting. There's no way he'll want these windows in anyone's hands but his."

"We lure him here into a trap and spring it on him?" Frank asked, looking impressed.

"Exactly. In Japan he has power and influence, but here, if we can catch him, he becomes just another criminal."

"I like it," Harvey agreed before standing up. "Frank, you're in charge. I want you to make this happen." Harvey walked toward the door. "Who is going to be Kortevan?"

Leslie looked at Frank, who looked back at him before shifting his gaze to Karl, who looked wide-eyed and surprised. "Me?" Karl asked.

"You're perfect. No one outside the office knows you, and if Kortevan has been described to Koshigawa, you look enough like him that you should be able to pass." Leslie saw Karl's doubtful expression, and Frank must have seen it as well. "I'll have your back." That seemed to reassure Karl, because he nodded.

Harvey asked to see Frank, and the two men left while the rest of the people in the room began making plans. Leslie was impressed at how quickly they came together once a decision had been made and a plan sketched out. By the time Frank returned, some of the details had already been worked out. Among other things, they'd also agreed to use a very roundabout way to let Koshigawa know he was being double-crossed. They spent quite a while strategizing, and by the end of the day, they had a detailed plan. Now all they needed to do was pull it off.

LESLIE yawned as the day kept getting longer and longer. The time change was definitely taking its toll, and he could barely concentrate as Frank finally indicated it was time for them to leave. "I don't think I can do this," Karl told Frank as the three of them walked to the elevator. "I don't have any experience with undercover work." He saw Frank place his hand on the other agent's shoulder.

"I know. That's why I'm going to go as your partner. I talked it over with Harvey, and I'm going to pose as Zvolensky. Koshigawa will probably be wary, but that's a chance we'll have to take." Leslie saw Frank wink at the other man. "Kortevan can explain that I'm his partner." Karl nodded slowly as some of the worry left his eyes. "Don't worry, I told you I'll have your back, and I will."

"So will I," Leslie added before he could stop himself. "If you do this, you'll be doing a great thing to help."

"I guess I can try," Karl responded, still looking a bit unsure.

"Good," Leslie said. "Tomorrow I'll start filling you in on everything I know about Koshigawa."

"And I'll get everything I can out of Zvolensky," Frank added with a determined set of his eyes and tone of voice before turning from Karl to look at Leslie. "I think we will together." Leslie nodded in response and saw Frank say a final good-night to Karl before pressing the button to call the elevator. "Don't worry," Frank reassured Karl before he and Leslie stepped into the elevator. Karl told both of them good night, and the doors slid closed, lowering the two men to the level where Frank had parked his car.

"Do you really think Karl is going to be able to do this?" Leslie asked, still seeing the doubt in Karl's expression. "He doesn't seem very sure of himself, and being effective undercover is 90 percent self-assurance."

Frank stopped for a moment before unlocking the doors to the car. "I think he'll be great. Karl's smart and resourceful. I think he'll pull off his part perfectly. I also think a touch of nerves will play well with Koshigawa. From what you've said, he'd expect people to be nervous around him." Frank unlocked the doors and got into the car.

Leslie followed suit, sliding into the seat. "I have to agree with you there. From all accounts, Koshigawa believes he can do what he wants and take what he wants. He would expect someone like Kortevan to feel a bit humbled and shaky in his presence, much like they would a god."

"Sounds like the man is a piece of work," Frank said, starting the engine and backing out of the parking space.

"He's a piece of something, anyway," Leslie retorted with a smile before settling back in the comfortable seat for the ride to Frank's house, his mind going a mile a minute even as his body wanted nothing other than rest.

THEY arrived at Frank's house, and Frank helped him bring up his luggage, which Frank placed in the guest room he'd used during his last visit. Leslie wondered if Frank had had second thoughts, but as soon as he set down the suitcase, Frank stood right in front of him. Within seconds, Leslie was pulled into powerful arms and kissed within an inch of his life. By the time Frank released him, Leslie was breathless and as hard as stone. All it took was a single kiss to transform him from jet-lagged and exhausted to excited. "We should get you something to eat and then to bed," Frank suggested quietly, and Leslie nodded, his throat dry. Frank kissed him again, this time with less energy, banking his inner fire for the time being, but Leslie could feel it ready to spring back to full flame at a second's notice. "Come on," Frank said before taking him by the hand and leading him out of the room and down to the kitchen, where Frank began to cook.

It didn't take him long to put together a simple but filling dinner, and they sat down across the small kitchen table from each other. They didn't talk much as they ate, but more than once Leslie felt Frank glide his hand over Leslie's where it rested on the table, each touch sending tingles through him and pushing back the weariness once again.

"Go on upstairs," Frank told him once they were done eating. "Get cleaned up, and I'll finish down here and join you."

Leslie nodded and got up, heading back upstairs. In the bedroom, he pulled out his kit and headed for the bathroom, where he brushed his teeth and started the shower. He'd been traveling for what seemed like days and felt sticky and dirty. Stripping off his clothes, Leslie pulled his hair free and stepped under the spray.

The hot water felt amazing on his skin, and Leslie let it wash over him, cleansing away the grime and sweat from the day. Reaching for the soap, Leslie stopped when he heard the bathroom door open and close. Then the shower door swung open, and Leslie's first instinct was to cover himself. That is, until he saw a very stunningly naked Frank step into the shower with him. Leslie moved his hands away from his groin and around Frank's waist as he was held tight.

Frank's mouth pressed to his in a clear communication that while they'd just had dinner, Leslie himself was dessert. The water rolled over both of them as Frank's skin slid against Leslie's, chest to chest, a strong leg spreading his legs apart, helping Leslie's raging erection slide along Frank's hip. The sensations of excited joy zinged along Leslie's spine, and he held on to Frank tightly as Frank stroked up and down his back before settling his hand on his butt, bringing the two men even closer together. "I love how you look wet," Frank told him between searing kisses that seemed to touch his soul. "I especially love how your hair slicks back." Frank kissed him again before stepping back and whirling him around. At first Leslie had no idea what was happening as he was pressed against the tile. His body and mind warred for a brief second until he felt Frank's hands soothe down his back, and lips lightly kissed his shoulders. "Just relax," Frank whispered from behind him as Leslie felt Frank press against him, his stiff cock riding along his crease. Leslie pressed backward and heard Frank chuckle into his ear. "I know what you want and you'll get it, I promise. But not quite yet."

Leslie groaned and practically willed Frank inside his body, pressing back harder, but he felt Frank move away and the water cut off. Frank pressed first one hand, then two against Leslie's inner thighs and Leslie parted his legs, anticipating whatever Frank had in mind, and he didn't have to wait long. Frank stroked a slippery palm down his butt, gliding between his legs before cupping his balls.

Leslie whined and whimpered softly, his legs shaking. "Frank."

"Press your butt back further," he said quietly, and Leslie complied, feeling lips against his butt as the hand slipped away. Leslie felt Frank part his cheeks and blow on his warm skin, sending a chill through his body, and he held his breath, waiting to see what Frank had in mind. "I'm going to make you scream," Frank told him as he slipped his hand away, and Leslie groaned as he was left wanting. The water started again, and Leslie jumped a little when soapy hands touched his skin. "Let's get you nice and clean so I can get you all dirty again."

Leslie turned and was pulled into Frank's tight embrace. "Why did you stop?"

"Because what I really want, I want to give you in a nice comfortable bed." Frank kissed him again and then stepped back, soaping his hands. Leslie sighed softly as Frank washed him. He giggled a few times when Frank brushed his fingers over ticklish spots. Once Frank was done with him, Leslie washed his lover in return. When they were done, Frank turned off the water and stepped out of the shower. When Leslie stepped out, he was immediately wrapped in a huge bath towel and Frank massaged his arms, chest, and back. Frank got out the hair dryer and turned it on. By the time Frank was done, Leslie felt completely pampered.

Once Leslie's hair was dry, Frank hung up the towels and led him by the hand to his bedroom. The windows were dark and Frank turned off the lights, a candle in the corner now the only light. "You're amazing, Frank."

"And you look like an angel by candlelight," Frank told him before taking Leslie into his arms.

Leslie's entire body vibrated with an energy he didn't know he had. Hell, energy his jet-lagged body shouldn't have came to the surface. "I love how responsive you are," Frank told him as a shiver rippled through him when Frank lightly circled a nipple with his finger. "You aren't like this with everyone, are you?" Frank asked, even though Leslie knew Frank already knew the answer. Leslie shook his head and gasped as Frank leaned forward, taking a nipple between his lips. "Just stand there for me," Frank whispered before tonguing his skin white hot. "I've waited weeks to see you again."

"Me too," Leslie gasped between clenched teeth. Their shower together had already stoked Leslie's fire, but Frank quickly built the stoked embers into a roaring flame. "I thought about you all the time," Leslie admitted as Frank stroked his hands over his chest. He could barely stand, his legs were shaking so much. "I thought I might have imagined the way we were together. You never called, and I thought you didn't feel the same thing."

Frank straightened up, their eyes meeting immediately. "I felt what you felt. But I don't want to talk about who didn't call whom, not right now." Frank continued gliding his hand down Leslie's skin, teasing the base of his throbbing cock before moving away. "I have more important things to say to you, but they don't need words." Frank kissed him hard, pulling Leslie into a tight embrace that left his vision swimming. "Lay down on the bed," Frank told him when he broke the kiss, and Leslie forced his legs to work, crawling over the covers to rest on his belly, his head buried in a pillow. Leslie felt a tap on his hip, and he lifted his head, looking into Frank's eyes. "Roll over, Les," Frank whispered, and he complied, still watching Frank's eyes. "Put your arms out and relax."

"What are you doing?" Leslie asked softly as Frank straddled his legs.

"Close your eyes and give yourself to me," Frank answered without providing an answer, but Leslie was too far gone to really care. Weight settled on Leslie's legs, and he waited, hearing the snick of a bottle and the smell of herbs. Then warm, oiled hands stroked over his skin, kneading to the muscles below. Leslie hadn't been aware of the tension he'd been carrying until his muscles began to release under Frank's incredible hands. Frank oiled and stroked Leslie's chest, doing amazing things to his muscles with his fingers. Leslie felt Frank shift beside him, and his legs and thighs got the same treatment. He'd actually begun to slip into a trance-like sleep when Frank pulled his hands away.

"Do you want me to roll over?" Leslie asked without opening his eyes—he felt too peaceful. Throughout the entire massage, every muscle in his body had relaxed, except one, and Leslie gasped, but kept his eyes closed as he was engulfed in hot wetness. His hips pushed forward, and Frank took him deep, sucking hard. Leslie had been wound up for what felt like hours, and it didn't take long for his brain to kick into gear. With a small cry, Leslie climaxed fast and hard into Frank's mouth.

His eyes still closed, Leslie could barely move as he let the afterglow bloom throughout his entire body. He felt Frank touching his skin, and it tingled with warmth. Once he caught his breath, Leslie opened his eyes and saw Frank beaming down at him, a pleased look on his face. "Want you," he said, and Leslie nodded, wondering how Frank wanted him, but too happy and relaxed to ask. Frank rolled him on the mattress and spread his cheeks, his tongue thrusting deep, and Leslie's mind awoke from its endorphin-drunk stupor.

"Frank, good God!" Leslie cried as he pressed backward, wanting more even as part of him cried it was too much. Leslie buried his face in the pillow, biting on the fabric as Frank began a second slow climb that he knew would ultimately reduce him to nothing. Tongue and fingers played his skin, lips adding an accompaniment to Leslie's moans and whimpers. Frank added his own melody on top of it all, and soon Leslie heard himself begging and pleading, for what he wasn't sure.

Leslie heard rustling and felt thick fingers breach him, then slip away, replaced with Frank's thickness, which burned so good as their bodies joined. Not content to wait, Leslie thrust backward hard, taking all of Frank in a single movement that stole his breath away, and Frank's surprised gasp filled the room. Leslie immediately rocked back and forth, forcing Frank deep. Then Frank's weight pressed him forward, and Leslie splayed on the mattress as Frank drove into him. Leslie arched his back, crying softly with each and every deep, soul-penetrating thrust. Frank's arms wrapped around his chest, holding them together, lips sucking on Leslie's neck as Frank pulled both of them higher and higher. Leslie felt sweat break out on his body, gluing Frank's skin to his as Frank's breathing echoed in his ears. Leslie wasn't sure how much more of this he would be able to take, and still Frank continued driving him higher as his cock kept brushing over the spot inside that sent waves of pleasure through him. The waves built on top of one another, and Leslie lost himself in it, letting Frank hold and guide him through it.

"*Frank!*" Leslie cried through his haze of passion as his second climax burst from his body. His head throbbed, and he clamped his eyes closed as the pressure in his head built to such heights he couldn't stop himself. He felt Frank's climax on the periphery of his consciousness, and it wasn't until Frank collapsed on top of him that Leslie fully registered what had happened.

They both lay in a heap, breathing and doing nothing else. Between Frank's weight and his own complete lack of energy, Leslie simply closed his eyes and let his mind float.

Frank slipping from inside his body made Leslie groan, and then he felt Frank's weight shift. Leslie whined softly at the loss of Frank's heat and the comfort of his mass. "You okay?" Frank asked him softly, and Leslie nodded, his hair falling into his eyes. Frank brushed it back with his fingers before kissing him gently.

"I'm fine," Leslie finally answered with a smile. "More than fine, actually." He rolled over and groaned when his butt hit the wet spot on the bed. "Sorry." Leslie felt a bit embarrassed, but Frank simply grinned like it was some great accomplishment. After getting off the bed, Frank helped him stand and pulled off the bedding, throwing it into the basket in the closet. Frank left the room and returned right away with fresh sheets. Leslie offered to help, but Frank had the bed changed so fast, he just stayed out of the way. Once the bed was remade, Frank ushered Leslie onto it before blowing out the candle and joining him on the fresh, crisp sheets.

Leslie rolled onto his side and closed his eyes, his body now so wearily tired that he could barely move. Frank almost immediately tugged him close, and Leslie smiled briefly as he thought about Frank watching over him as he slept. Leslie didn't think about it much, though, as his weariness took over and he almost immediately fell into a deep sleep.

LESLIE woke to light from the windows in his eyes and a warm sensation on his skin. Cracking open his eyes, he saw Frank grinning up at him from where his head rested on Leslie's belly, lips kissing his skin. "It's about time you woke up," Frank teased, his eyes dancing with mischievous delight. Leslie watched as Frank returned to kissing his skin. "You know you taste really good," Frank said, punctuating his comment with a long lick across Leslie's belly.

Leslie sat up, and Frank lifted his face, bringing their lips together. Leslie used the opportunity to press the bigger man back until he was laying catty-corner on the bed. Now it was Leslie's turn to feast his eyes and lips. "You say I'm sexy, but when was the last time you looked at yourself in the mirror?" Leslie asked before swiping his tongue over a light-brown nipple.

"I'm just me," Frank answered, and Leslie felt his face being tugged toward Frank's.

"Uh-huh," Leslie agreed, not buying the modest bit, but then Frank kissed him again, and he gave up his argument. He felt Frank trying to turn them on the bed, but Leslie resisted, holding Frank's hands tightly. "You've seen to my pleasure more than once."

"Not about keeping score," Frank chided lightly and tried again, more forcefully, turning them on the bed.

"No. But it is about trust," Leslie retorted and saw a dark shadow pass across Frank's face. It lasted only a few seconds, but it was there, and Leslie wondered what had caused it. Before he could ask, Frank pressed him into the mattress and began feasting on his neck. Leslie began to squirm in unabashed delight and forgot about anything else. In fact, Leslie had the feeling that the only thing either of them thought about for a while was the taste of each other's skin and the sounds they both made on this delightful morning that continued out of the bedroom and into the shower. It seemed to Leslie that Frank couldn't get enough of him, which was just perfect, because Leslie knew he would never tire of the man's touch.

Once they finally got out of the shower, they pulled on their clothes. Frank took a look at the clock, and they rushed out of the house, Frank driving like a demon through traffic to the office. "We'll be late for Harvey's meeting this morning," he explained as Leslie held on for dear life and hoped he made it to the office in one piece. After they came to a squealing halt in a parking space, Frank rushed them to the lift, only stopping once they were on their way upward. "Sorry," Frank said with a grin when he saw Leslie heaving for breath.

Leslie smacked Frank on the rear end. "That's for scaring the life out of me on the drive." The elevator door opened, and Leslie watched him school his expression. Leslie closed his eyes and did the same, sad to let the happiness he'd experienced go, but they didn't need to post an advert about their feelings.

"Hey, Karl, any news?" Frank asked as they approached the desk.

"Yeah. Our message got delivered and word came back through one of Leslie's people that Koshigawa apparently threw an urn across the room. It seems we've gotten his attention, anyway, but he's not going to be particularly happy with Kortevan, um... er... me."

Frank looked concerned, and Leslie saw his gaze shift between the two of them. "Maybe we should rethink this," Frank said to both of them. "It's not too late."

"It's fine," Leslie said, and both men stared at him. "Koshigawa isn't a mobster. He's a businessman who's used to getting what he wants because he has piles of money, and he's used to using that to his advantage. It just means we have his attention. If we'd have gotten word that he hadn't reacted, then we would need to worry, because that would mean he wasn't going to take the bait."

"He's right," Harvey said from behind him, and Leslie started slightly, not realizing he was there. "But so is Frank. I think we need to evaluate who is going to play Kortevan. Karl, you've done a superb job on this case, but I don't want to put anyone in any unnecessary danger." Leslie looked at Karl, and he could almost see the man's face fall. Sure, he might have been nervous, but Leslie remembered his first undercover assignment. While he'd spent most of the preparatory time half scared to death, when the time came, he was ready and pulled it off beautifully. Leslie could see Karl behaving the same way when he got the opportunity, and now his chance was flying away.

"If I may be so bold, can we not overreact to this?" Leslie began, and saw both Frank and Harvey turn, with Frank glaring daggers, which surprised him. "We were all convinced that Karl could do this yesterday, and suddenly because we got news that our quarry reacted as we hoped he would, that has us scared? I think we're all better than that." Leslie kept his voice calm and level, but he wanted to reach over and smack the look off Frank's face. Harvey nodded and looked thoughtful but didn't say anything before turning and walking back toward his office. Karl looked uncomfortable and sat at his desk, hiding behind his computer. Finally, Leslie turned to Frank, whose lips were nearly white, and his jaw appeared clenched so hard Leslie expected Frank's teeth to explode. Finally, he tilted his head toward a conference room, and Frank turned and walked inside, apparently waiting for Leslie to follow.

As soon as he was inside the room, Leslie heard the door bang closed. "Don't you ever contradict me in front of my boss again! I'm in charge of this operation, not you, and I'll make the decisions that are best for the team."

Leslie felt his own anger rise, and his instinct was to punch Frank in the jaw, but there would be repercussions for that. And with the way Frank looked right now, the man would probably start an international incident. "Just a little full of yourself, aren't you?" Leslie asked between gritted teeth. "Or maybe you're simply the biggest arse I've ever met in my life!" Leslie stepped closer. "I don't know what's gotten into that thick head of yours, but knock it off! Because I have to tell you, if what I see in front of me is the real Frank Jennings, then I know the man I woke up with this morning is never laying a hand on me again!" Leslie turned and saw everyone in the office looking at them through the glass walls. "Yesterday I saw you treating Karl as an equal, willing to give him a chance to prove himself, and now at the first little sign, you pull it away from him. What kind of fucking partner are you?"

"Now hold on here!" Frank yelled.

"No, you hold on, Mr. Scaredy-cat. You were all kind and sweet until we stepped out of the car, and now you're acting like some big-bollock-headed Neanderthal. I don't know which Frank is the real one, but let me tell you this, until I do, you're not touching me again. And another thing, you owe that man an apology. He was willing to go undercover because you asked him to. Now he's wondering what in hell he did wrong. You think being a man is about being in control? Being a man is about being who you are, not making everyone scared of you." Leslie took a deep breath, holding Frank's eyes, daring him to say a word. "And one more thing: if you think just because you fucked me a few times that you can push me around, you're dumber than you look." Leslie pulled open the door and walked out of the conference room, banging the door closed behind him. He made it halfway across the room before he realized that everyone was watching him with their mouths hanging open. "What?" he asked the room, and they all turned away and went back to work.

"Les," Karl said quietly from his desk. "Umm, I don't know how to tell you this, but Frank forgot that room isn't sealed." Karl looked up, and Leslie followed his gaze, realizing that the walls stopped about a foot from the ceiling. Leslie looked back at Karl, who was now doing his best to stifle a laugh. "You know, I think half of us have been waiting for someone to stand up to him, and you did it in spades."

Leslie looked into the conference room and saw Frank staring back, looking completely humiliated, and Leslie's anger and frustration died away in a split second. He looked over at Harvey's office and saw the man hard at work, or at least he was pretending to be, and after a while, Leslie saw him look up, meet Leslie's eyes, and nod his head before returning to work. Leslie decided it was best to let Frank deal with things on his own, so he sat at Karl's desk.

"Koshigawa is old-school Japanese. He's into honor and respect, but he thinks everyone should just honor and respect *him*. He doesn't necessarily return it. So when you meet him, keep your eyes lowered slightly unless you feel you need to challenge him to make a point. Then look him square in the eye and don't back down."

"How long do you think it will be before he gets here?"

"It could be just a few days. The quicker he arrives, the more it means he wants his prize."

"I've alerted customs, and they're keeping an eye out for him," Frank explained in a soft voice as he walked over from the conference room. He looked somewhat subdued, but there was still a fire burning beneath his eyes, and Leslie tried to think of something that would soothe his hurt feelings, but he could think of nothing. "We also have someone at the desk at the Pfister Hotel. If Koshigawa does come to town, he's sure to stay there." Frank seemed all business right now, and Leslie didn't push it.

"How do we make contact with him?" Karl asked a bit nervously.

"We don't. As soon as we get word that Koshigawa's in town, we'll move you to Kortevan's apartment and let him make contact with you. Mr. Kortevan has reluctantly given his permission, thanks to Harvey."

"So I'm still going to be Kortevan?" Karl asked warily.

"Yes," Frank answered, his eyes meeting Leslie's, and Leslie knew that was probably as close to an apology as Frank was capable of. "So now we need you to pick Les's brain so you know as much about this man as possible."

CHAPTER 5

FRANK seethed beneath the surface as he did his best to keep himself under control. He hated not being in control, and maybe he'd overcompensated because they were at work, but they needed to behave in a professional manner, especially when they were in the office. Frank made sure he listened to what Leslie was telling Karl even as his own thoughts whirled through his mind. To Frank's surprised frustration, Leslie seemed to be acting as though nothing had happened, including the man telling everyone in the office about what they'd been doing in bed. That was no one's business but theirs. "Just keep your head and you'll be fine," Leslie was telling Karl. "Frank will be there as backup, and I'll be close by, as well, listening in, with every word being said recorded." Frank forced his attention back to the work and away from his whirring thoughts.

"Will he have people with him?" Karl asked.

"Probably," Leslie answered before looking to him, and Frank nodded his agreement.

"We'll be sure to meet in a semipublic place and will have people around," Frank told Karl, realizing that some of what Leslie had told him was right. Karl had done very well on this investigation, and he deserved this opportunity. Frank could see the eagerness in Karl's expression as he soaked in everything Leslie had to say like a sponge. "You're going to do great," Frank told Karl and then sat at his desk. He checked e-mails for any reports from customs, not that he was expecting anything yet—it was too soon. As he was clearing the rest of his e-mail, his desk phone rang. "Frank Jennings."

"Agent Jennings, this is Brian Watson. I was just calling to follow up to see if you'd had any luck on the case."

Frank thought a few minutes, an idea forming. "There's something I'd like to discuss with you about that. Would it be okay if we came to your office?"

Frank heard typing. "I have an opening in my schedule in an hour," Brian answered.

"We'll be there," Frank answered and disconnected the call. He looked over at Karl and Leslie, still talking earnestly. Damn, Les was sexy as hell, especially with his hair down. Frank had to give the man credit—he wasn't afraid to stand up to him. Sure, Frank hated it. He was used to using his weight and influence to get what he wanted, but he had to give Les credit for not backing down, and the man was certainly hot when he was angry. The fire in his eyes was something to see, even if he did piss him off to no end. Karl and Leslie stopped talking and both of them turned toward him, and Frank motioned them over. "I got a call from our burglary victim, and we have an appointment with him in less than an hour. We'll leave for his office in half an hour."

"Okay," Karl answered before returning to his desk, but Les said nothing. Frank noticed that he was back to glaring at him, and that was fine. If Les was still angry with him, he could deal with that.

"I shouldn't have raised my voice at you," Les said before turning away, following Karl to his desk. Frank shook his head and returned to his computer screen, trying to ignore the occasional looks from the other people in the office. He had work to do, and it needed to get done. A few minutes before leaving, Frank informed Harvey where they were going.

"Take Interpol if you like, but I need Karl to follow up some things here in the office. You can bring him up to date when you get back," Harvey told him, and Frank nodded before leaving Harvey's office, muttering softly to himself. He'd been hoping to bring Karl so he wouldn't have to be alone with Les. The last thing he wanted to do was talk about his "feelings" right now.

He needn't have worried. Riding down in the elevator and on the walk to Brian's office, Les didn't say a single word. Part of Frank was grateful, but another part missed their conversation and the way Les's blue eyes looked at him, but his pride would not allow him to be the one to speak first. So they walked through the warm, sunny streets in a dome of silence. Frank checked his watch as they approached the building and noticed that they were a little early, so he sat on a bench in the sunshine to wait a few minutes, looking straight ahead.

"Jesus Christ, Frank," Leslie said. "I know you're angry, but you don't need to act like a spoiled child."

"Me?" Frank hissed. "My sex life is all over the office because of you. How am I ever supposed to look them in the eyes again? It's bad enough that you questioned my decision, but that...."

"I did not question your decision, I gave a different opinion. That's what I'm here for, remember? Or did you just want me here as your sex toy?" Leslie added softly, but with a hint of venom. "You don't need all this macho crap. It's like a chip on your shoulder, and quite frankly, it's not attractive." Les's expression softened, and Frank saw beneath the anger to a flash of hurt. "What's the real you?" Les stood up and checked his watch before looking toward the front doors of the office building. With a near silent sigh, Frank stood up and led the way inside.

In the lobby of Brian's law firm, Frank gave his name to the receptionist, and to his surprise, Brian came out himself to get them. Brian led them to his office and closed the door, offering both him and Les a chair after Frank made introductions. "So, what is it you'd like to speak to me about?" Brian asked, clearly curious.

"We did catch the men who broke into your house, and we also recovered the windows from the Milwaukee Conservatory of Music. None of this has been publicized because we believe a large collector from Japan is involved," Frank explained, and Brian nodded vigorously.

"If we catch him red-handed, we're hoping to cast international doubt and pressure on his entire collection," Les added. "Is there anything in your experience that could help us in dealing with the Japanese art laws? I've had dealings with them in the past, but you may have some other insight."

"The only loophole we've ever encountered is when the buyer knows the art is stolen. That's the key. So you need to get your suspect to admit that he knew he was buying stolen goods. Their law heavily presumes a lack of knowledge is innocence in these cases." Brian leaned back in his chair. "Make sure you do everything by the book and get him dead to rights. Because as soon as you arrest him, he'll hire the best lawyers he can find and bring international pressure."

"I know," Frank answered.

"If there's anything our firm can do, let us know. We'll help any way we can," Brian offered, and Frank stood up.

"Thank you for your time, you helped confirm a number details for us." Frank looked at Les, who nodded his agreement. "Say hello to Zoe and Nicolai for me."

"I will," Brian said with a smile. "Zoe is still talking about her tour." Brian shook hands with both men, and they left the office, heading toward the elevators. Frank felt pretty good about the meeting, and Brian had confirmed his suspicions. His lighter mood lasted until the elevator doors closed and Les stared back at him as though waiting for an answer.

"The real me is the man you saw last night," Frank said, answering Les's question from earlier.

"Then why the whole asshole routine?" Les asked.

"I'm not being an asshole; I'm just being professional in the office. If I wasn't tough, they'd walk all over the gay guy," Frank explained.

"You confirmed that Karl is gay, and they don't walk over Karl. They treat him with the respect his knowledge deserves, and they'll treat you the same way if you do the same," Les said before turning away again. "Sorry, it's none of my business, and I won't say anything about it again. Tonight after work, I'll get a car and move my things to a hotel. That's probably best for both of us." The doors opened, and Les strode out of the elevator toward the front door of the office building. Once they were out on the street, Frank caught up with the strong-willed Brit.

"I thought you had more in you than that," Frank retorted, and Les stopped walking.

"What's that supposed to mean?"

"It means I thought you had more fight than that. You stood up to me, but now you're running scared. So I can be a bit of an asshole sometimes, and I know I'm a control freak, I have been since—" Frank stopped himself from going there.

"Since when?" Les asked, and Frank sighed and shook his head, pushing the memories back behind the walls. "I didn't know everyone could hear what I said. That was meant for just you. But you should have known...." Les paused. "You did know, and you figured you could take me in there and give me a dressing down that everyone would hear to establish your dominance. Instead, it backfired, and now you've got your bollocks in a twist about it."

Frank took a deep breath, because Les was damn close with that observation. "You didn't have to tell everyone about our private business," Frank retorted weakly.

"At least I told them you fucked me. Your fragile macho ego should still be intact." Leslie turned and walked toward the federal building without turning around. Frank watched him go for a second before shaking his head and striding to catch up. This whole thing was getting way out of hand.

"Les, do you think we've had enough of this 'mine is bigger than yours'?" Frank asked, and Les turned, looking at Frank like he was going to argue again.

"It's mine." Then Les smiled, and Frank realized just how silly and pigheaded they'd both been.

"We'll see about that," Frank retorted, "later."

"Frank," Les cautioned.

"I know I'm pigheaded and controlling."

"I think I've shown I can handle that," Les said as they resumed walking back toward the office. "It's not that any of what's between us really matters. Once this case is over, I'll go back to London, and you'll still be here. There's no escaping that. We can fight like cats and dogs and bugger each other until we collapse, but that fact isn't going to change. Either we nail Koshigawa to the wall or we don't, but either way I fly home." Les turned and resumed his walk to the office. This time Frank let him go. He'd been so happy to have Les back with him that he hadn't thought beyond tonight. People walked around him on the sidewalk, and a man bumped into him, spurring him forward. He walked fast and saw the door to the building close as he approached. Pulling it open, he showed his badge to the guard and walked toward the elevator, stepping in as the door began to close.

Les stared back at him, and Frank pulled the other man to him, kissing him as hard as he could as the car rose. The car began to slow, and Frank released Leslie from the embrace. "You can't tell me that doesn't matter," Frank whispered as the doors slid open. "And for the record, you are not and never were a sex toy or anything else. And what you felt last night and two weeks ago was real." Frank left the elevator and walked to his desk, leaving Les behind in the elevator. He didn't want to turn around, but in his mind's eye, he could see Les touching his lips.

"Did you two kiss and make up?" Karl asked from his desk as Frank approached, looking alternately at each of them. "Because you've both got just-kissed lips." Karl snickered before returning to his screen.

"Jennings," Harvey called from his office door and made his way over. "It looks like your quarry has taken the bait. The FAA reported that Koshigawa's company filed a flight plan for their private jet to fly from Tokyo to LA and then on to Chicago before coming here. He's probably somewhere over the Pacific now, so you need to make sure everything's ready for first thing tomorrow morning." Harvey went back into his office, but not before lifting his eyebrows slightly. "Karl's right," he added before shutting the door.

Frank pushed the comment and everything other than the case from his mind as he walked back to his desk. He gathered the team and told them Harvey's news. Everyone got to work, and Frank pulled open his desk drawer, getting out his gun. "Grab yours too, Karl. We keep them on us from now on." Frank slid the desk drawer closed with a bang. "Let's get over to Kortevan's apartment so we can set up and make sure all is ready. We aren't sure how soon after arriving Koshigawa's going to try to make contact, but we can assume he's going to do it in an attention-getting way." Frank stopped and looked at Les. "Are you coming?"

"Yes," Les responded, and they all headed for the elevator. Frank threw Les a set of keys.

"Those are Kortevan's, or at least they were. Since the vehicle was used in the commission of a crime, we impounded it. Follow me over, and we'll park it in his spot so it's visible. Let people think he's home and everything's normal." Frank was pleased with preparations so far, and together the three of them left the office.

Frank drove carefully, knowing Les didn't know his way around town, and he also figured the man was trying to get used to driving on the right side of the road. It took longer than usual, but eventually they pulled up to Kortevan's apartment building on the west side of town. The building was brick with six apartments in it. Frank parked around the corner and motioned Les into a spot visible from the main road. Using the keys, they unlocked the back door and walked inside. The apartment was on the first floor, running from the front to the back of the building. "At least we have two exits," Karl said as he wandered through the rooms.

"The man was a terrible housekeeper," Les commented, and began picking up clothes from off the sofa with the tips of his fingers.

"There's a clothes basket in here," Karl said, and Les retrieved it and began throwing the loose clothing off the floor into it before stuffing it into the back bedroom.

"You should see that room, it's full of crap. Is it stolen?" Les asked, and Frank shook his head.

"The bureau has been through here thoroughly. It appeared he kept his goods in the storage locker," Frank said, and he saw Les open closet doors and close them again. At least the room didn't look so trashy anymore, but even so, Karl and Les continued cleaning the worst of the mess. Frank wandered from room to room, checking the layout of the apartment, noting all the windows and the view from each one. "If you two Nancy Neatnicks are done playing maid, we can get down to business," Frank said as he walked back into the living room. He might have teased them, but the place did look better and definitely smelled better already.

"What do we have, Frank?" Les asked after placing a wad of paper towels in the trash.

"Front and back door, large windows looking out the front, and smaller side and back windows. There is a blind spot near the corner of the building. Someone could sneak up from the street at night, so we'll need to pay attention to that."

"As I was cleaning, I checked out the kitchen. There isn't much there, but I placed all the knives in a drawer so they wouldn't be standing out on the counter," Karl said.

"Very good. Did you learn where everything is? I once had an undercover operation go bad because the suspect asked for a spoon and the agent didn't know which drawer to open. The suspect immediately knew something was off and bolted," Les offered, and Karl hurried back to the kitchen, opening each drawer and cupboard and memorizing the contents. "Do the same thing in the bedroom and bathroom. This is your apartment. It doesn't matter that you wouldn't be caught dead actually living here, Koshigawa has to believe this is your place."

"Les is right. You should also start dressing the part: old jeans and faded shirts. You can't look like you're expecting company. Kortevan would have no idea Koshigawa is coming, so he'd be going on with business as usual, and you need to do the same thing."

"What about the neighbors?" Karl asked.

"In this area, nobody knows anyone, and they don't stay around for very long if they can help it," Frank answered, impressed with the way Karl was throwing himself into this assignment. "This is your last chance to back out, Karl."

"I'm Dale, Dale Kortevan," Karl said before turning and heading back toward the bedroom.

"I think he's going to be fine. The truth will come when he hears from Koshigawa," Les explained, and Frank agreed.

"We need to get these cameras and bugs set up and tested."

"Do you think Koshigawa is really going to come here?" Les asked skeptically. "He would never be caught dead in a place like this."

"Maybe so, but he'll probably send someone to check things out and maybe even put a touch of fear into good ole Dale, and we'll want to get everything we can on audio and video. We'd bug his hotel room, but we really don't know where he's staying. We can only guess." Frank retrieved the equipment he needed from the trunk of his car and returned to the apartment. Karl wandered back into the living room from what appeared to Frank to be the back bedroom. "I've been thinking, we may need to sleep here for a night or two," Frank said, and he saw Karl pale slightly. "Did you check out the bedroom?"

"Yeah. The place is a sty." Karl walked toward the kitchen and began looking under the sink, coming up with a couple spray bottles and a roll of paper towels. Then he headed back down the hall, grabbing the vacuum as well.

Frank opened the bag and began laying out the equipment. "We'll place a mic in each room, and I think we can probably cover most of the apartment with a few cameras. I'm also going to see if I can place one in the hallway as long as I'm not observed." Frank held up the small, lipstick-sized camera. "Are you familiar with these?"

"Sure," Leslie answered, and Frank saw him move down the hallway, looking all around him. "There's a vent at the end of the hallway that might work." Leslie picked up one of the small cameras and a screwdriver, walking down the hall while Frank began setting up the camera in the living room. There weren't many possible locations, but he found one after a few minutes and got it placed. Then he booted up the laptop in the case and checked the signals from the cameras and the view he was getting.

"Looks good," Frank told Les when he returned. "We're getting almost the entire hallway and living room." Les looked over his shoulder, and Frank felt the slight touch of his hand. The tension from earlier in the day seemed to have dissipated between them, but Frank still didn't know how Les really felt about him. Sure, they'd settled their disagreement, at least on some level, but Les's words about being off-limits still rang in his ears. Regardless of those words, Frank's heart rate sped up just from Les's simple touch. Then the hand slipped away, and Frank felt its loss like an ache.

"We should get the rest set," Les told him before picking up another camera and heading toward the back bedroom. Frank couldn't help glancing at the computer screen, watching Les as he sauntered down the hallway. He actually gave Frank a smile before entering the bedroom.

They worked easily together for the next hour, setting everything up and making sure it all worked. "That's the last of it," Frank said with a smile as Les walked down the hall from planting the last listening device in the extra bedroom. "Everything seems to be working." Frank checked his watch, realizing just how late it was. "Damn," he said softly as a thought sprang into his head.

"What is it?" Les asked from where he was triple-checking that nothing they'd done was visible.

"You were right," Frank told him.

"About what?" Les's eyebrows raised in what Frank read as curiosity.

"I am different in the office, and I feel different when I'm in the office. We've been working here all afternoon, and not once did I think of how others might be looking at me. I've been sort of relaxed." Frank looked up at Les, meeting his eyes. "Why didn't I see it before? Why didn't anyone tell me?"

Les actually chuckled at him. "You didn't see it because you're too close to it. And as for someone telling you, I somehow doubt you've ever let anyone at work get close enough that they'd actually get to know the real you, so how would they know there's a nice guy under the intimidating exterior they always see? The people in the office are part of your team, and I suspect they'll respond to you the way Karl has, if you let them." Les turned away and began packing up the equipment. Frank helped, and they heard the vacuum cleaner run at the far end of the apartment. "I bet you're not listening to bugs right now. That would probably blow your ears off."

"Yes, it would," Frank agreed as he packed away the laptop and wandered off to find Karl, who was vacuuming the floors with a vengeance. "Whenever you're ready," Frank said, and Karl kept moving.

"Five minutes," he answered, and Frank chuckled to himself, but left Karl to it. Since he was going to be staying here too, Frank figured he could leave Karl alone and let him make the place habitable.

Once Karl had turned off the machine, they packed and left the apartment, leaving Kortevan's truck in its parking space and riding back to the office. "Tomorrow morning, we'll get to Kortevan's place early, and that's where we'll stay until we're contacted. The crew will be monitoring everything from an electric company vehicle about half a block away. If anything happens, we can have backup in less than half a minute," Frank explained to both Les and Karl once they were in the now quiet office. "Come dressed like Kortevan, and I'll do the same. Les is going to be riding along with the support team." Frank turned toward Harvey's office and then back to Karl. "Go on home and get some sleep. You're going to do just fine."

"Thanks, Frank," Karl answered with a nervous smile before grabbing his things and leaving the office.

"I'll be right back," Frank told Les, and then he walked to Harvey's open office door, knocking on the frame. "Everything's all set. Is there any news?"

"Our quarry landed in Los Angeles. There's no word on when he's leaving, but we'll keep an eye on him."

"We're planning to go to the apartment in the morning."

"Good. Let the neighbors see you and think you're new tenants. They'll be less suspicious that way." Harvey gave Frank a small smile and nod before turning off his light. "Go on home and rest. The next few days are going to be long and tedious." Harvey stood up and grabbed his bag. "Keep me informed," he added before walking through the office to the elevator.

Frank returned to where Leslie waited for him. "Let's go." Leslie grabbed his things and followed him out. Frank could almost feel the man's gaze on his backside the entire time.

DOWN in the car, Frank placed their things in the trunk, got in the car, and pulled out of the parking space. He drove through town and parked near a small restaurant. After getting out, they walked toward the door. "Best Italian in town," Frank explained, and once inside they were greeted by the owner, an Italian grandmother who'd been running the place for over twenty years. "Frankie, where have you been?"

"Sorry, Nana. I've been working," Frank answered as he returned her loving hug. "Les, this is my grandma, Josephina. Nana, this is Leslie. He's working with us." Frank didn't go into any details on purpose, and he saw her looking from him to Leslie and then back.

"It's nice to meet you," Leslie said as he shook Nana's hand. At first Frank wasn't sure how she was going to react. Nana could be very old-fashioned, and when he'd told her he was gay, she'd pretty much ignored it, after making the sign of the cross, of course. She also seemed to see everything, and even as an adult, Frank had a very difficult time keeping anything from her. Nana would make an excellent interrogator.

"Come, eat," Nana said, taking Les by the arm and leading him toward a table. "You're too skinny." Frank shook his head and followed the two of them. Once they were seated, Nana motioned one of the servers over. "Tina will bring you drinks, but you don't need to order. I'll make something special."

"Thanks, Nana," Frank answered, and his grandmother walked back to her station as more people entered the restaurant. Tina, a tall blonde, took their drink orders and then hustled away.

"Your grandmother seems very nice," Les said as he sipped his water.

"Nana's great. Opening a restaurant was Pappy's dream, and they ran it together for a number of years. After he died, my parents thought she should sell and retire, but she loves it. And I know the only way she'll stop is when they carry her out of here. The way Nana feels, she isn't serving food, but love on a plate." Frank took a drink of his own water and watched as Nana motioned one of the servers over before walking into the kitchen.

"Where are your parents?" Leslie asked. "Do they live here too?"

Frank shook his head. "They retired and moved to Florida. Nana's not my real grandmother. She's my step-grandmother. My father's mother died, and Pappy married Nana when my dad was in high school. She was younger than Pappy by about ten years, if I remember right; my dad's only twelve years younger than she is. She and Dad didn't speak for a long time, but they get along now. Dad always resented her, and he can be a real stubborn ass when he gets a notion into his head." Frank noticed that Leslie lifted his eyebrows, but had the grace not to say anything. "I guess I come by it honestly."

"As long as you admit it," Leslie said with a smirk.

"I don't really remember my mother's parents. They both died when I was young, and Pappy's been gone for almost ten years, so the only grandparent I know is Nana. And since Mom and Dad moved, she's the only real family I have in town." Frank smiled as he saw Nana poke her head out of the kitchen and then disappear inside again. Tina brought their drinks and then hurried into the kitchen, returning with a tray of plates, antipasti, and a huge salad. She set both on the table and put plates in front of each of them. They both thanked her, and then Frank placed some of the salad on his plate. His grandmother's homemade, tangy salad dressing brought back memories the way it always did. She'd made it for as long as Frank could remember, and she swore the recipe was dying with her. It wasn't on the restaurant menu and was reserved almost exclusively for family.

"This is amazing," Leslie exclaimed as he took a bite of salami rolled so tightly you swore you could use it as a toothpick. "Did Nana teach you how to cook?"

"She tried, but I could never sit still long enough to really learn from her," Frank explained, and he continued eating as he watched the gustatory joy show on Leslie's face.

"I haven't had food like this since the last time I was in Italy," Leslie said after swallowing another bite. "Let me amend that. I didn't taste food like this when I was in Italy." Leslie ate another bite of the salad. "This is amazingly wonderful," he said with his mouth full before covering his lips with his napkin and swallowing. Frank stared across the table, watching Leslie eat. After working on the police force and now for the FBI, Frank had learned to eat fast, but Leslie ate with a mannered grace that Frank found fascinating. Hell, he found almost everything about Leslie fascinating.

"What's your family like?" Frank asked, setting down his fork and taking a sip of his beer.

"It's just my mum and me now. I barely knew my dad. Mum says he was a real wanker, and I can barely remember what he looked like. She says she's getting near retirement now and she's trying to decide what she wants to do. She keeps talking about going to Spain, where it's warm, but I doubt she'll ever leave England."

"What does your mother do?" Frank asked, loving the way Leslie's eyes warmed when he talked about his mother.

"Have you ever heard of Carlton Elite?"

"You mean the chain of high-end bath products Nana loves so much? Of course—I go there every year to buy Nana's Christmas presents. Why?"

"That's my mum. She started the company after my dad left, making the products at home and selling them herself. Now she sells by appointment to the queen. Mum says she's going to retire, but I think she's got a lot in common with your nana. She loves what she does. I know she'd love it if I came into the business with her, but I'm not really interested," Leslie explained as he finished the last of his salad and reached for more, refilling his plate. "I know she worries, but I love what I do." Leslie continued eating and polished off another plate of salad as well as at least half the antipasti plate. "I've died and gone to heaven."

Frank couldn't help smiling as Leslie complimented Nana's food. He knew that would endear him to her, as would the fact that the man could put away the food. Tina arrived at the table and took the dishes as the kitchen door opened and Nana came out carrying a tray. Frank was about to get up when Leslie set his napkin on the table and pushed back his chair, meeting Nana as she crossed the room. He took the tray from her, and to Frank's surprise, she let him. Leslie carried the tray to the table, holding it for Nana. "I made gnocchi with pesto," she said proudly. It was her special dish, and Frank's favorite.

"It looks amazing," Leslie said, setting the tray to the side. He sat back down, and Nana served out huge portions for each of them. Then Nana leaned to Frank and lightly kissed his cheek.

"This one is nice. Not like that Mark." Nana shook her head. "Didn't like pesto. Bchh!" Then she turned and walked back toward the kitchen, and Frank watched her leave.

"Who's Mark?" Leslie asked once Nana was out of earshot. "Is he the thing you said we'd talk about later?"

Frank nodded. "But it's not late enough, and I haven't had nearly enough to drink." Frank gulped half his beer and thought of asking for another one, but it would only get back to Nana and she'd scold him. Besides, he had to drive.

"What did he do to you?" Leslie asked quietly after taking a bite of the gnocchi and sighing softly. "Your Nana could win cooking contests with these." Frank had thought the food might distract Leslie from the uncomfortable subject of Mark, but no such luck. "Talk about it and you'll feel better," Leslie said.

"Are you a psychologist too?" Frank asked, and he saw Leslie reach across the table and then stop as if he'd suddenly realized what he was about to do.

"No. I'm willing to listen, though."

"I'm not sure I'm willing to talk. It's not something I'm very proud of." Frank took a bite from his plate, but the food had lost most of its flavor, and Frank set down his fork with a clink and reached for his beer once again. Even that didn't taste good anymore. Frank looked down at the plate of comfort food and shook his head. This could not be happening. It wasn't until he felt Leslie place a warm hand on his that Frank looked up again. Leslie didn't keep his hand there long, but the touch was reassuring.

"Mark is my ex-boyfriend. Actually, at the time, I thought of him as my husband. We dated for a while and then made our relationship permanent, or at least I thought it was permanent." Frank's thoughts raced in every direction, and he tried to keep them focused, but emotions he'd kept buried down deep all tried to get out at once. "We were serious for about three years. We had an apartment and we'd furnished it together. I thought at the time that we were going to be together forever. I should have known better. Nana hated him, and I thought it was because she hadn't accepted me as gay. Nana can be pretty stubborn." Frank knew he was rambling, but the thoughts didn't want to form a cohesive whole, and now that he'd started, everything tried to come out at once.

"Frank, what happened?"

He took a deep breath and stopped talking for a minute to give his thoughts a chance to settle. "During the time that Mark and I were together, I was working homicide for the Milwaukee PD, and Mark worked in information systems as a project manager. My life was chaotic, and I only seemed to see the worst of what society had to offer. As I said, we were together for three years, and as a project manager, he traveled a lot. There were times when he was away more than he was home, but I knew that when I met him."

"The travel became too much?" Leslie asked softly.

Frank figured he should just go for broke so all the noise in his head would simply quiet. "Mark was on a trip to San Francisco and had an extended weekend, so I flew out to surprise him. It was me who got the surprise, when I called him once I'd landed and asked him where his hotel was. All I got was a lot of hemming and hawing. So I called a friend at the bureau, and they traced his cell phone signal to an apartment in the Mission. It seemed that I wasn't the only guy who thought Mark was their one and only. The kid in San Francisco was just as shocked as I was when I knocked on his door and found Mark trying to explain what was going on."

"You mean…?" Frank saw Leslie gulp and his eyes widen. Frank looked for the pity he expected to find, but all he saw was anger.

"Yeah. The kid threw Mark out, and I flew back to Milwaukee and called a few sympathetic friends on the force. We evicted Mark from the apartment and my life for good. For three years I thought he was the one, and he'd been playing me the entire time. I trusted him with everything in my life."

"How long ago did you kick him out?"

"About two years ago, I guess." Frank felt wrung out. "I never thought about it as a breach of trust, but that's what it was. It's hard to trust other people, but it's also hard to trust myself, because I was so wrong before.

"Do you trust me?"

"Yeah, but...," Frank began and didn't quite know where to go with the statement so he stopped trying.

"Go ahead and eat," Leslie told him softly. "I don't want Nana to think I'm taking away your appetite." Leslie smiled, and Frank picked up his fork.

He couldn't take his eyes off Les, staring at him as he tried to figure him out. Les seemed to be able to read him like a book, and Frank wasn't too sure how he felt about that. He hadn't known Les very long, but damn, if the man could read him that easily... it was definitely a bit disconcerting.

"God, you should see yourself," Les said from across the table, chuckling softly. "No, I cannot read your mind, and you really aren't that easy to read. We're not that different." Frank waited for Les to continue as he took a bite of Nana's cooking, letting the warm richness of the comfort food slide down his throat. "Do you think I don't know how others see me? I know I'm good-looking. I had one man tell me I was the prettiest man he'd ever seen. About five years ago, one of my mum's marketing geniuses wanted to use me in some of their adverts. Mum actually thought it would be a good idea, but that's not what I want. Since I was sixteen, everyone has looked at me as a pretty face."

Frank listened and looked at Les's "pretty face," wondering what was wrong with looking good. And again, Les seemed to read his thoughts.

"I had my first boyfriend when I was at university. He was sweet and really kind. Or I thought he was. But all he really wanted was a pretty young man on his arm. He loved to show me off to his friends, but that's all I was to him." Les ate slowly, his expression deadly serious. "I never knew if people liked me for me or because of my looks. I know it sounds self-centered, and lots of people would like to look like me, but it's hard to trust people when all they think of you is arm candy or how I'd look in bed." Les lowered his eyes to the plate and began eating. Frank wasn't sure what to say, so he remained quiet. After a while, Les's fork clinked on the plate. "On the last night at Cambridge, I went out to a gay pub with some friends. We were having a good time, and I saw a bloke looking at me from across the room. He was *really* looking at me. When he came over, he had this voice like warm honey and he asked me to dance." With a story like this, Frank expected Les to smile at the memory, it sounded nice, but his eyes were as hard as granite. "We danced together for a while, and then he bought me a few pints and we talked and then danced some more. He said his name was Oliver and that he was shipping out with the Royal Marines in the morning."

"I take it he was feeding you a line," Frank prompted once Les stopped speaking.

"One of my friends heard Oliver's mates talking in the loo, and Oliver had made a hundred-pound bet that he could bag the prettiest guy in the place before midnight."

Frank risked a small smile. "I take it he wasn't successful."

"No. My pals wanted to make them pay, but after they told me, we all left and went back to Cambridge, and I got monumentally pissed." Les continued eating. "So you're not the only one who has a hard time trusting sometimes."

"Then why me?" Frank asked. "Why did you come to my room that night?"

"Honestly?" Les asked, and Frank nodded. "I thought you were sexy and I was attracted to you. I knew that I was probably going to leave soon, so you were safe in a certain way. I had no idea that you would completely blow my mind, or that you would touch me in a way no one else has." Les looked around the room and then leaned over the table. "I had no way of knowing I would think about you for weeks afterwards, wondering if you were thinking of me too. I felt like such a girl, but I couldn't help it. And for the record, I trust you, for some reason. I know you think of me as more than just my looks."

"You're a smart man, Les, and you deserve to be thought of that way. You're also damned sexy, especially when you're...." Frank heard Nana's voice behind him, and he stopped his thought midsentence. Frank could feel his cheeks heating, and he hoped Nana had not been listening to his conversation.

"You're not eating, Frankie," Nana said, and Frank leaned back in his chair and took a bite from his plate to make Nana happy.

"This is incredible, Josephina. I was just telling Frankie that this is better than the food I got in Italy." Les gave Nana one of his high-wattage smiles and patted his belly happily.

"I'm glad," Nana said, beaming. "You boys finish up while I bring the dessert."

Frank barely stifled a groan as Nana walked to the kitchen. "It's surprising that I'm not 800 pounds," Frank complained with a smile. He loved his nana, and he loved her cooking.

"Does she always feed you like this?"

"Every time I come in here, and at home, she's worse," Frank warned, but he stopped as he saw Nana carrying a tray to their table.

"My own special version of tiramisu," Nana explained as she set a plate in front of each of them, with three small dessert portions on each. "I know it's probably sacrilege, but I like tiramisu with chocolate. The ladyfingers are underneath with the mascarpone mixture on top, and I serve it in a chocolate cup."

"I love these," Frank said, popping one of the bite-size morsels into his mouth. "Now, these she does serve here in the restaurant," Frank told Les proudly. "They're one of her best sellers." Frank saw Nana beam, especially when Les ate all three of his in rapid succession while making the appropriate appreciative noises. Once they were finished eating, Frank argued with Nana the way he always did over the bill for dinner and ended up giving the money to their server before saying good night to Nana and heading back toward home.

THE day had been long, and Frank was more than happy to see his quiet house. Pulling up in front, Frank parked, and they walked quietly inside, settling in the living room after Frank got a bottle of wine and two glasses. Unlike the evening before, Frank wasn't sure quite what to expect, and he waited for Les to give him some sort of indication, but nothing was forthcoming, at least not for a while.

"Look, Frank, I'm not sure what we're getting ourselves in for," Les began, and Frank felt him shift on the sofa.

"I know," Frank agreed. "But you're here now, and I'm willing to let that be enough. I'm not going to ask for undying love or declarations shouted from rooftops." Although in his heart of hearts, that was indeed what he wanted, but he couldn't acknowledge that to himself, let alone Les. Frank set his wineglass on the table beside the sofa. "I don't know about tomorrow, but I want you here with me for as long as I can have you. If that's a day or a week, I'll take it and live with it." Les sipped his wine and appeared to be thinking. "I'm not saying I don't care, because I do, but we have to be realistic." Frank swallowed as he tried to find the words to explain what he was feeling. He wasn't doing this right. "I know you'll have to go back when this is over, and I'll understand if you want to leave things and just move to a professional relationship. I'll understand and respect that, but it's not what I want."

"And what do you want?" Les asked, and Frank leaned close, his hand carding through Les's silken hair, tugging him slightly as he kissed him. The rich taste of the wine mixed with undertones of the flavor that Frank knew was all Les, and that was what he was after. Shifting on the cushions, Frank pressed Les back onto the sofa, guiding him down as their kiss deepened. Les settled his hands on Frank's back and then slid lower, settling on his butt, gripping through Frank's pants.

"Damn, you taste good," Frank whispered when he came up for air, but he didn't wait for Les's reply before devouring him once again. Briefly, Frank thought of moving to the bedroom, but his body had very different ideas, and it seemed Les did as well. Les moved his hands from Frank's butt, and then Frank felt Les opening his shirt. Breaking the kiss, Frank sat up and nearly ripped the fabric as he pulled off his shirt and then tugged at the buttons of Les's. Once he saw skin, Frank latched onto a nipple, licking and sucking on Les's skin. He tasted like heaven, and Frank could not get enough. Les shook slightly beneath him, and Frank felt him arch his back. Frank increased the pressure, fingers working at Les's belt. Les made the most amazing little noises, which only spurred Frank on. He loved those small mewling sound that Les made deep in his throat. Sometimes he sounded like a cat.

"Frank," Les gasped as Frank parted the fabric of Les's pants, freeing his cock from its fabric constraint.

"What is it you want?" Frank asked, and Les rolled his head back against the armrest, pushing his hips forward. Without waiting for a verbal answer, Frank licked a swipe down Les's heavy length and heard a high-pitched squeak, then a moan that shot right through Frank. Smiling to himself, Frank looked into Les's glazed eyes. "You only act this way for me, don't you?" Les did his best to nod as Frank took in the decadent sight as he sat up. All laid out on the sofa, alabaster chest against dark fabric, pants open, hips thrusting, Les was the very definition of hedonism. "I know what you want," Frank said as his eyes drilled into Les.

Getting off the sofa, Frank kicked off his shoes before shedding the rest of his clothes with as much speed as he could muster. Les's shoes thunked onto the floor, and by the time Frank was naked, so was Les. "Want you, Frank," Les said, his voice deep with need.

"I know." Frank grabbed Les by the hand and hauled him to his feet. He nearly took it further and lifted Les off his feet to carry him up the stairs fireman-style, but he managed to stop. Still holding Les's hand, Frank practically dragged him up the stairs and into the bedroom before pushing him onto the mattress.

Les landed on his stomach, which was fine with Frank, because he pressed himself to Les's back, letting warm, smooth skin slide against his. Kissing his way down Les's body, Frank tongued Les's lower back just above his butt, and Les thrust backward for him, bringing that bubble butt into perfect position. Frank knew he drove Les crazy when he ate him out, and that was exactly what Frank wanted. Listening to every sound Les made, Frank ran his tongue along Les's crease, tasting his lover as his own cock jumped with every sound Les made, and the man made the most decadently hot sounds Frank had ever heard.

"Damn, you're hot," Frank told Les before probing deep, listening for the telltale high pitches, which he'd learned meant Les was being driven out of his mind. Les's unique flavor burst onto Frank's tongue as he licked and teased the puckered opening. Working a finger into Les's tight opening, Frank saw his lover arch his back. The cries began when Frank found the small bundle of nerves just inside, and Les threw his head back, his long hair whipping onto his shoulders. God, he was gorgeous. Frank smoothed his hand down Les's butt, stroking the warm skin as he pulled his finger free, licking and sucking the sensitive skin.

"Frank, don't want to wait!" Les growled, and the last of Frank's willpower snapped. Frank grabbed a condom from the drawer and rolled it onto his cock. Positioning himself at Les's entrance, Frank pressed forward, entering his lover with a long, slow stroke. "God!" Les hissed through clenched teeth before making sounds Frank wasn't sure a human being should make. Frank reveled in the sensation of Les's body around him. Nothing he'd ever done had prepared him for the deep connection he felt with Les right now. Pressing deep, Frank sank into his lover as far as he could and waited, holding still, feeling Les's heartbeat and wondering what he was going to do when Les left.

That errant thought made Frank gasp, and thankfully Les thought it was passion and began to move beneath him. It wasn't hard for Frank to push his thoughts aside, especially when Les began to move, and Frank withdrew slowly. Frank watched as more of his cock slid from Les's body, his skin dark in comparison to Les's alabaster paleness. Then Frank drove forward, Les's heat pulling him back in like a siren song. Rubbing his hands down Les's back, Frank gripped Les's slender hips and held them both still, listening to his lover's moans as his cock jumped inside his lover. He wanted to stay like this forever, joined with Les so deep he'd never have to let him go.

"Don't tease me, Frank," Les told him as he tried to move. Frank had barely been hanging onto the last of his control, and Les's whimpery tone broke the last of it. Snapping his hips back and forth, Frank took them both on a journey of passion. Frank's head throbbed and his body sang as he let go and gave Les everything he had. Through a daze of desire, Frank could hear Les's cries and moans, but they seemed so far away, like Les was already leaving him. Then a massive cry rocked the walls, and Frank felt Les tense around him, and he knew Les was climaxing. The thought pulled him right along behind.

Frank held Les, breathing like he'd run a sprint as he lightly kissed Les's shoulder. "You're amazing, you know that?" A soft chuckle reached Frank's ears, and he felt Les move beneath him. He slipped from Les's body as his lover rolled beneath him, and then Frank was being kissed hard while Les held him tight. "If we can move, we should probably get cleaned up before bed," Frank said, and Les nodded before letting Frank up.

Hand in hand, they walked to the bathroom. Frank started the shower and they both got in, caressing and washing as the water soothed and cooled sensitive skin. Once clean, Les dried his hair, and Frank straightened up the bedroom. Getting into bed, Frank turned out the light and held Les close. His body completely exhausted, Frank should have fallen to sleep immediately, but his mind refused to quiet. All he could think about was how good it felt to have Les with him and how empty his bed was going to feel when he left.

CHAPTER 6

TWO days. Two whole stinking days. Les's legs ached and his rear end throbbed from this bollocking chair inside the van he'd been stationed in since they set up surveillance. And damn the thing stank. Frank and Karl were in the apartment, and Les could hear his lover's voice every time he spoke—even when he whispered. They'd had no word on Koshigawa. Harvey had told them he'd landed in Chicago nearly two days ago, but there had been no contact or even anything that might look out of the ordinary. Les was beginning to think this was a fool's errand and their quarry wasn't coming after all.

"Frank, just checking in," Jim, the man in charge this shift, said into a microphone. Regardless of whether anything happened, they all checked in with each other every few minutes just to be sure nothing was amiss. It seemed ridiculous, since they could hear that Frank was all right, but they did it anyway.

"We're good. Playing Monopoly in here. There's nothing on television, and we're already tired of these filthy walls," came Karl's answer, and Jimmy smiled. Every time he checked in, Karl made some crack about the apartment. Anything to relieve the boredom, which grew with every hour. Leslie heard Frank's voice as well, and the tone of disappointment and frustration definitely came across the wire. Leslie was well aware that all of these people knew that patience was key, but they'd been at this for two days already with no word that any of it was doing a damned bit of good. A phone rang in the van, and Leslie answered it since Jim was busy at the moment.

"This is Carlton," he said after picking up the phone.

"Les, where's Jim?"

"He's making updates," Les explained, instantly recognizing Harvey's voice. It wasn't one anyone tended to forget—Leslie figured he'd remember it for the rest of his life. "Is there any news?"

"It looks like our quarry isn't coming. His pilot filed a flight plan back to LA for this evening," Harvey explained, and Leslie could feel the disappointment settling into his stomach. He'd thought for sure that they were so close this time.

"Should we pack it in here, then?" Leslie asked, and he saw Jim look up from his screen with an equally disappointed expression.

"There doesn't seem to be much point in continuing," Harvey answered, and Leslie knew he was right. After handing the phone off to Jim, Leslie sighed and rested back in his chair. His supervisors were not going to be happy that he'd come all this way on a fool's errand, but this had happened before, and it would happen again. Many of the cases his art-recovery division worked came to nothing, and many took years of dead ends in order to bear fruit. Leslie knew he had to file this away along with everything they'd learned and hope for a better resolution in the future. Jim talked to Harvey for a while longer and then hung up the phone.

"He wants us to stay here for a few more hours and then pack it in. Harvey doesn't think they've taken the bait, but he wants to play it safe."

"Could all this be a load of crap?" Leslie asked, half thinking out loud. "I mean, if you were traveling somewhere to purchase something that wasn't exactly legal, you'd send everyone who might be looking for you on a wild goose chase. That's what I'd do, and probably what Koshigawa would do." Leslie's mind whirled with possibilities, but he wasn't sure any of them were worth anything. He'd learned a lot about the man over the years. "If I were him, I'd send my plane somewhere like LA, but I wouldn't be on it."

"What makes you think this Koshigawa wants these windows that badly?" Jim asked without looking up from his computer screens and monitors, which showed Frank and Karl playing a game on the living room floor.

Leslie stood up, the van way too small to contain his sudden burst of energy. "The man's obsessed. And as far as we know, he's never specifically pushed to have a specific item stolen before. Up to now, he was only a buyer. He doesn't want any loose ends, and he wants those specific windows. I don't think he's going to give up or come all this way to go home empty-handed. Remember, Hiro Koshigawa is used to getting what he wants, especially from people he considers inferior to himself." Leslie paced with baby steps in the tiny space. "We have to give this a little more time."

"I don't know if Harvey is willing to do that," Jim said, and Leslie agreed, checking the time. It was already late in London, but he dialed a number and waited for an answer.

"This better be good," the voice on the other end answered.

"It is. That message you delivered a while ago for me."

"Yeah," Leslie's contact answered warily.

"Follow it up with another that the seller has found another buyer," Leslie said, listening to a woman's voice in the background.

"Okay, but this makes us even," the man said.

"We'll never be even unless you do for me what I did for you, and you know it," Leslie said roughly, and Jim turned to look at him, his eyes widening. Leslie heard the woman's voice again, and the line went silent before disconnecting.

"Who was that?" Jim asked, and Leslie shook his head.

Leslie thought about not answering at all. "A contact, and you heard nothing at all," he replied, and Jim nodded, then turned toward the monitors. "I need to speak with Frank and I do not want that conversation recorded." Leslie put on the electric company jacket and hat. "He and I will be taking a walk. We'll be gone for no more than ten minutes." Leslie opened the van door and got out, closing it behind him before striding down the block and up to the front door, where he pressed the call button. The door buzzed, and Leslie walked inside and up to the apartment door, which opened right away. Leslie said nothing, but took off the jacket and helmet, tossing them onto the chair. Then he walked down the hallway and out the back door, with Frank following behind. He didn't care that they were on video; Leslie just did not want to be overheard.

Pushing open the back door, they left the apartment and stepped outside. "What's going on?" Frank asked as soon as the door closed.

Leslie walked to the sidewalk, and Frank went along. Leslie wanted to be away from the building. "I had a friend, the one who helped us earlier, put out the word that a sale was imminent."

Frank's eyes narrowed. "Before, you made it sound like your team did it."

"I can't go into details, but I have sources that no one knows about, and you don't, either." Leslie put up his hand. "Don't ask any questions, because I won't answer them any more than I'd ask you to tell me about your confidential sources. My source is going to turn up the heat."

"Why now?" Frank asked, but Leslie knew he already knew the answer. "We're running out of time, aren't we?"

Leslie nodded as they kept walking. "Can you blame anyone?" he asked, keeping his voice low. "You've already recovered the windows and caught the actual thief. Sure, they want the big fish, but they'll settle for what makes their record look good, and closed cases do that. Besides, your supervisors can make a big deal about how they recovered the windows, especially when they're reinstalled. They were never going to let this go on for much longer. Hopefully my contact will be able to deliver a message quickly."

"Should I tell Harvey?" Frank asked.

"No. Only if you have to. If it works, it works. If it doesn't, there's no harm done." Leslie turned and walked back toward the apartment building. "I told Jim we wouldn't be gone long, and he's going to be getting nervous. We'll know by the end of the day, I hope."

Frank nodded his agreement, and they said nothing more as they walked. Inside the apartment, Leslie walked to get his coat and hat. Karl sat watching television, but Leslie could see the questions Frank wanted to ask plain in his eyes. Leslie wanted to say something, but he knew Frank couldn't actually ask his questions any more than Leslie could answer them, not with everything said in the apartment sent to the truck and recorded for posterity. Lingering for a few seconds by the door, Leslie looked into Frank's eyes, trying to convey what he wanted him to know. Then he turned and opened the door.

"Thank you for all your help," Frank said for the benefit of anyone who might be listening.

"It's no problem. Call us if anything else happens," Leslie answered before leaving the building and walking back to the truck. Once inside, Leslie took off his costume and hung the stuff up. Jim got out, and then Leslie heard the engine start and the vehicle moved for a few minutes before stopping again. Then the door opened and Jim climbed inside, closing it quickly behind him. Leslie placed his phone on vibrate and settled in to listen and hope.

Stakeouts take time, but Leslie knew the hardest part was remaining vigilant for hour after monotonous hour. The only excitement they'd had all day were the two additional times they'd moved the truck and the UPS man delivering a package that they intercepted. All they got was a box of big-boob porn, which they rewrapped and Leslie placed outside the apartment door. The last of the sunlight faded and Leslie snuck out, grabbing a terrible American fast-food dinner for both him and Jim before returning to the van. By then Frank and Karl were playing some sort of video game, laughing and challenging each other. "Is anyone relieving you?"

"No. Harvey sent me a message before he went home that we were to pack it in and come into the office tomorrow morning." Jim yawned and sat back in his chair, opening the bag Leslie had brought back for him. They both ate and didn't say much. Leslie and Jim had basically been cooped up together for going on three full days. They'd exhausted most of what they could talk about. After eating, they gathered the trash and settled in for a long night of waiting. "Go ahead and nod off," Leslie told Jim. "I'll watch for a few hours and wake you if anything happens."

Jim agreed, and after a few hours, Leslie woke him and took a few hours to catch some sleep. After spending so many hours awake, he easily fell to sleep, even sitting up. Jim woke him later, and Leslie took the next shift, spending hours listening to Karl snore like a lumberjack. Leslie turned down the volume and opened the van door to let in some fresh air. Closing it after a few minutes, Leslie caught a glimpse of someone moving near the apartment.

"Jim." He shook the man's shoulder, and he jumped awake. "There's someone near the shrubs. This could be it." Leslie felt completely awake, energy coursing through his body.

Jim immediately jumped to the microphone. "Frank, Karl, there's someone outside, be on your toes." They heard Frank answer softly, and a few minutes later Karl did the same, albeit a little more sleepily. Jim monitored all the equipment, and Leslie got his gear ready in case the guys needed back up.

A loud rapping on the apartment door made both of them jump. Another pound, and then they heard Karl open the door. "Yeah."

"You Dale?" a male voice with an Asian accent asked briskly, and Leslie saw the man step into the apartment on the hallway camera.

"What are you doing?" Leslie heard Karl ask, and then he heard what sounded like a punch. On the monitor, Leslie saw Karl double over and Frank walk forward and then stop.

"You have something boss wants," the man said in what sounded like broken English. Karl was still struggling to stand upright, and Leslie had to admire that both men hadn't caved, although Jim looked as though he were ready to rush in there like a cowboy.

"It's okay," Leslie soothed in a whisper. "They're doing fine. He needed to deliver his message from the boss." Jim calmed down and narrowed the camera to get a good picture of their visitor's face. Definitely Asian, and the man was definitely strong. He looked like he was going to hit Karl again, but both Frank and Karl backed away and looked like they were afraid.

"Unless you want more," he said as he dropped a card on the floor, "be there with the goods at eight." The man grabbed a floor lamp, pulling off the shade and skewering the television before leaving the apartment and walking out of the building. Leslie quietly opened the van door and watched as the man got into a dark sedan and pulled away. Leslie committed the plate to memory and then went back inside. Grabbing a sheet of paper, he wrote down the plate while Jim conversed with Karl and Frank.

"Karl's going to be fine," Leslie heard Frank say.

"I am not," Karl squeaked. "I think I lost my lunch."

"You did not," Frank countered. "You kept your cool and played the part perfectly. Now all we need to do is get ready for a meeting in a few hours. Call Harvey and fill him in. Karl and I need to continue to play our parts until the meeting, in case we're being watched." Frank held the card up to the camera so they could get a look at the address. "Let me know what he says and we'll make plans from there."

"They said to bring the merchandise. They'll be expecting Dale's truck," Karl added, his voice sounding a little less pained.

"We'll let Harvey know," Jim said before closing the lines of communication and immediately calling Harvey. They had a spirited conversation before Jim handed the phone to Leslie.

"What's the plan?" Harvey asked him.

"I need you to give Frank and me an hour. We need to talk, and we haven't been able to up till now," Leslie explained.

"You already have an idea, don't you?" Harvey asked.

"Yes, but I need to talk with Frank first." Leslie knew if he simply went ahead and did what he thought was best, Frank wouldn't be happy. After all, this was Frank's operation.

"One hour," Harvey said and disconnected. Leslie handed the phone back to Jim, wondering where in the hell Americans learned phone etiquette.

Leslie pulled off his shirt and rummaged in the small bag he'd brought. Most of the things were dirty after two days, but he found an old T-shirt, pulling it on along with a pair of gym shorts. "What are you doing?" Jim asked, staring at Leslie's preparations.

"We need to assume they're being watched, so I want to look like a co-conspirator who was called in a panic in the middle of the night." Leslie took off his trainers and socks, then slipped his feet back into the trainers but didn't lace them. Then he tied up his hair and shoved it down the back of the shirt before pushing open the door and getting out.

He took a roundabout route and came up on the apartment, walking briskly in his disheveled state. The lock on the outer door had been broken, and Leslie went inside, knocking softly. When the apartment door opened, Leslie stepped inside and closed the door. "We have less than an hour," he told the two of them. "Harvey's orders. I have a plan, but we need to put it together fast." Frank nodded for him to continue. "The two of you are going to need to be at that meeting," Leslie said, and Frank nodded, while Karl didn't look so convinced.

"It's too late to back out now," Frank told Karl as he patted the other man on the back. "We need to see this through."

"I know," Karl answered with more conviction than was written on his face. "What's the plan?"

TWO hours later, Leslie stood in the office waiting for Frank and Karl, and he was definitely getting worried. They should have been there a while ago and hadn't shown up yet. "Give them a few minutes," Jim told him, and Leslie was about to call Harvey again when both men walked through the door. "Sorry," Karl said when he saw them. "We were tailed and had to lose them."

"I made sure there was no one else," Frank explained. "Let's get the truck loaded. We only have a few hours before the meeting."

"It's already being loaded, Frank," Harvey explained as he walked toward them. "Just relax and make sure you all know what you're supposed to do." Harvey looked at all three of them. "I want all of you wired up for sound."

"They're going to check," Leslie began, and then he turned to Harvey. "What do you mean all of us?"

"If they were following Frank, then they saw you go into the apartment, so you're going with them. Now get ready to go after we get the wires in place. I've already got men getting into position around the warehouse. I don't want anyone taking any chances, and if things start to go bad, get the hell out of there." Harvey went to his office, and Leslie followed Frank to another department, where they were each given a small microphone.

"Harvey, they're going to search all of us. We aren't going to be able to wear wires." Frank said, placing the microphones aside.

"These you can," Harvey countered and handed each of them a small ring. "Put them on your fingers. The batteries only last a few hours, and they don't have the range of a larger device, but they should do the job. Now get some rest for a few hours before you head over to the warehouse. I want you all fresh and ready so we don't have any mistakes." Harvey continued on to his office.

Leslie wondered where they were supposed to rest, but Frank led them out of the building and into the nearest hotel, where he paid for a room. Inside, they found two double beds, and Leslie crashed onto one with Frank resting behind him, an arm around his waist. Karl took the other bed, and Leslie knew nothing more until a loud alarm sounded a few hours later. Leslie felt better when he woke up. He knew that feeling wouldn't last forever, but he hoped they'd all had enough rest to be able to pull this off. Getting up, they took turns showering before dressing mostly in what they'd been wearing and heading back to the office.

Leslie and Karl waited by the truck, which was loaded with the boxes that contained the windows, while Frank went up to check in with Harvey one last time. When he returned, they got into the truck and headed for the meeting.

The ride was nearly silent. Leslie could imagine that each of them was as deeply immersed in his own thoughts as he was. Frank drove, and Les sat in the middle between him and Karl. To say butterflies danced in his stomach was an understatement. Leslie had not been mentally prepared to go along, and he was still trying to get his mind around the sudden change of plan. He understood Harvey's reasoning, and he couldn't find a flaw with it, but it was taking him some wrangling to get his mind to settle on the task at hand. Thankfully, from years of experience and training, Leslie pushed away all thoughts other than the operation they were on. He knew that his life would depend on Frank and Karl, just as their lives would depend on him. That thought alone was enough to clear his mind and allow him to focus.

"We still have some time," Frank said and made a turn down a narrow street. "A few wrong turns should help us lose anyone that might be following us." Karl turned to look behind them, as he'd been doing for most of the trip. "I haven't seen anyone, but it's good to make sure. I also want to give us a few minutes to talk." Frank pulled the truck into what looked like an old, disused parking space, leaving the engine running.

"This should be simple, right?" Karl asked. "We get them to admit what they're doing and then we arrest them."

Leslie smiled, and he saw Frank do the same. "Nothing is ever that simple. Keep on your toes and keep your eyes open." Frank turned to Karl. "You've done a great job, and all you need to do is play the part you've been playing for the last few days. Don't get cocky or overconfident. Remember, you're a guy who stole these windows, and he's the buyer. What you want is the money, and when he hands it over, we have him."

"Koshigawa isn't likely to admit much to anyone," Leslie explained. "This isn't the movies where the bad guy reveals his whole plan once he has his nemesis in his grip. They want to get their goods and get out of there as quickly as possible, with a minimum of sound or anything that will draw anyone's attention."

Frank nodded his agreement to what Leslie had said. "Keep your cool no matter what happens, and watch your back and ours." Frank smiled to his partner before pulling out of the parking space and driving the rest of the way to the old warehouse.

The building looked as though it hadn't seen any life in years. Graffiti covered the outside walls, and the windows were all boarded up. As they approached, there was no sign of movement. Frank pulled in and parked near a set of doors and waited. All three of them looked at one another, wondering if anything was going to happen. Frank turned off the engine and got out of the truck. Leslie watched as he looked around and then walked to a door, checking it before turning back to the others with a shrug. Walking back to the truck, Frank got inside. "We give it five minutes and then we leave." Leslie could tell that Frank was nervous, even though his voice did little to reveal it.

After another few minutes, an overhead door began to lift, and all three of the men looked at one another. Leslie could tell that Frank was not keen on driving inside, but their only other choice was to leave, and that wasn't what they'd come for. Leslie saw the man he'd seen in the monitor last night motion them forward, and Frank started the engine, slowly pulling the truck into the warehouse. Leslie knew there were many things that could go wrong, and all of them were being set up right now. Once they were inside, Frank shut off the engine and opened his door, getting out of the truck as the overhead door slid down, blocking out a lot of the light. Leslie and Karl got out as well, watching as the man they'd already seen was joined by two walls of flesh and muscle. "You have something for me," a smooth voice from behind them said, and a man in a fine suit stepped around them. Leslie instantly recognized him.

"Yes," Karl answered. "Your offer was too good to refuse." He shifted slightly on his feet. "You have the money?"

Koshigawa nodded and motioned to one of his associates, who set a cheap case on the floor. "I want to see the windows." Koshigawa's men stepped toward the truck, and Karl looked to Frank, who instantly pulled a gun.

"Not so fast," Frank began. "Dale, check the case and make sure it's all there. No one moves until we make sure." Karl stepped toward the case, his legs a little wobbly, and Leslie saw Koshigawa's men pull guns as well.

"Let's keep things calm," Leslie said, doing his best to try to cover his accent.

"That's right," Frank said. "We just want to make sure everything is here before we give you the windows." Karl opened the case, and they all saw the money. Karl closed it again and looked briefly at the others.

"It's all here," Karl said, which was supposed to be the signal for the others to move in, but nothing happened. Leslie could see the expectation on Karl's face for just a brief second.

"Let's get these crates off the truck, and then you can see what you purchased," Frank said, playing for time, and he stepped back as two of Koshigawa's men stepped forward. Koshigawa's men waved their guns, indicating for them to move, and not having a choice, they backed away from the truck. The Japanese men gently lifted the first crate off the truck, and Leslie could see the avarice on Koshigawa's face as he approached it. The other two were removed as well and set on the concrete in a row. Leslie was well aware that they were quickly running out of time as he watched Koshigawa stare down at the crates like a man who'd just walked across the desert and was now looking at a huge pool of cool water.

Leslie continued backing toward the door, and he saw Frank and Karl doing the same thing. There was no way they could make it out with Koshigawa's men so close, and all Leslie could think was that they needed to get the hell out of here right now.

The sound of wood scraping wood echoed through the warehouse as one of Koshigawa's men pried the lid off a crate. The three of them continued inching toward the door, and Leslie wondered where the other men were. Koshigawa snapped an order in Japanese, and his men all came to an immediate halt. Then he leaned over the crate, and the three of them walked toward the door, their guns still in their hands. Leslie felt the cold knob under his hand when he heard another order, this one barked loud and fast in Japanese. Leslie spun around, his gun still in his hand, and found himself staring into the faces of Koshigawa and at least eight of his men. "You did not think I came prepared for a double cross?" he said as two of the men approached. Leslie looked at Karl and Frank and realized they were vastly outnumbered. Sure, they'd shoot some of them, but in the end there were too many, and the three of them were going to die. Their only saving grace was that Koshigawa still wanted his merchandise. A shot rang out and Karl danced. He appeared unhurt, but a chip in the concrete right near his foot showed just how close he'd come. "I want my merchandise," Koshigawa said in the same measured tone, but glass shattered as Koshigawa stomped onto the contents of the crate.

"Too bad," Frank said as he stared back at the men. "You aren't going to get them." The gig was obviously up, and their minutes numbered. "We're federal agents, and you're all under arrest. Everything you've said has been recorded, and we have great pictures of your man there from last night. Put down your weapons and surrender peacefully." Frank was putting on quite a performance, and for a second it looked as though Koshigawa was thinking about it.

"I do not think so," Koshigawa countered and pointed toward the ceiling. "Radio scramblers. No one can hear anything, and with you dead, no one ever will." Koshigawa stepped behind his men as the doors burst open and men swarmed inside.

"Lay down your weapons!" echoed off the walls as the words blasted from a bull horn. Leslie breathed a sigh of relief, watching the other agents approach Koshigawa's men as they lowered their weapons. But then a shot rang out, followed by another, and Leslie saw Frank and Karl dive for cover behind the truck. Leslie did the same thing, taking a running leap to safety behind the vehicle. Leslie hit the pavement and rolled, reaching the shadow of the truck, lying on the ground as more shots rang in the cavernous space. Then all was quiet except for men shouting orders and the moaning of others who'd been hit.

"Is everyone okay?" Harvey's familiar voice called out, and Leslie heard Frank and Karl answer. Leslie tried to, but he couldn't seem to get any air.

"There's blood back here," Karl called, and Leslie heard him rush away and Frank move closer. Leslie rolled onto his back, and Frank gasped. Leslie felt a hand glide into his. He tried to say something to comfort Frank, after all how bad could it be, since he didn't feel anything at all.

"We need an ambulance," Frank called, his voice sounding very unsteady. Leslie tried to get up, but Frank kept him where he was, and soon others joined them. "You're going to be okay," Frank said, and he continued holding his hand. "Hang on and stay with me," Frank told him in a whisper, and to Leslie's surprise he realized that Frank was very near tears. He tried to tell him it was okay, but the world began to get fuzzy and all watery. "Please stay with me, sweetheart," Frank said when Leslie closed his eyes, and he let the words bounce around his head before opening his eyes once again. Frank's eyes shone back at him, filled with fear and concern. Leslie wanted to remind Frank that he was essentially at work, but then he didn't really care. Sirens sounded outside, and Leslie heard more hurried footsteps, and then lights were being shone in his eyes and people crowded around him. Through it all, he felt Frank's hand in his. That light touch grounded him, and whenever he opened his eyes, he looked for Frank's—rarely were they absent. People asked questions, and Leslie ignored them, not having the energy to answer.

The world around him narrowed, and Leslie wanted more than anything to close his eyes and go to sleep, or whatever it was that felt like sleep. The only thing that stopped him was the feel of Frank's hand in his. Leslie's entire consciousness wrapped itself around that touch. He felt himself moving and heard voices around him, but it was the feel of rough fingers entwined with his that kept him from letting himself float away. "Stay with me, sweetheart," Leslie heard Frank plead, and he tried to tell him he would, but there were things in the way now, and Leslie didn't have the will or the strength to fight them. It took all his strength to hold Frank's hand, all his concentration to make his fingers move and tighten around Frank's.

Leslie felt as though he were floating, and opening his eyes, he saw what looked like movement around him. Closing them again, Leslie held Frank's hand as voices continued around him. Then he felt Frank's fingers slip from his, and Leslie felt his final hold on the world slip as his mind, no longer grounded, drifted away.

CHAPTER 7

"HAS there been any word?" Karl asked as he approached the hospital waiting room carrying two cups of coffee, and Frank stopped his pacing. He could not sit still no matter what he tried to do. "I brought you decaf," Karl said as he handed Frank one of the cups. Frank glared at him until he realized Karl was joking.

"No. They won't tell me a thing, and I've done everything but threaten to arrest the nurse at the desk," Frank glared at the woman, who paid him no attention as she continued her work.

"Did they say anything?" Karl sat in one of the chairs, and Frank gave up the ghost and sat as well.

"Just that the doctor was with him, and they'd be out to let me know. That was a while ago, and I haven't seen anyone." Frank sipped from the cup and continued glaring at Nurse Ratchet behind the desk.

"Agent Jennings? I'm Dr. Kraft." Both Frank and Karl stood up. "I'm sorry it took so long to get back to you, but Mr. Carlton is not doing well, and it's taken all this time to get him stabilized. We've prepped him for immediate surgery. He's very weak, and quite frankly, we're not sure he has the strength to make it, but it's our only hope. I need to get back, but I'll let you know as soon as we have anything."

Frank collapsed into the chair like his legs had been knocked out from under him.

"What are his chances?" Karl asked, and Frank simply nodded.

"I wish I knew. He's a fighter for making it this far. All we can do is hope he continues to fight," the doctor answered before walking away. Frank felt as though someone had stolen the oxygen from his lungs. He tried to breathe, but nothing seemed to work. Finally, he heaved a breath and clamped his eyes closed as tight as he could. This could not be happening. His last mission had resulted in someone on the team being shot, and now Les was lying in an operating room, and no one had any idea if he was going to survive.

"This wasn't your fault," Karl said as if reading his mind.

"I know it wasn't my fault!" Frank said too loudly and with too much force. Karl cringed and then stared down into his coffee cup. "Sorry. I'm worried about him."

"You're more than worried, and it's okay to admit it. It's okay to have feelings for him, and it's okay to be scared that you might lose him," Karl said softly, and Frank glared at him, but Karl simply shook it off. "Everyone knows how you feel about him. Half the department heard you call Les sweetheart more than once, and they all told me to give you their best."

Frank looked around the empty waiting room and wondered just how much their good wishes were worth. The only one there was Karl. Frank stared blankly at the walls and held his cup of coffee, wishing time to pass so he would know if his lover was going to live.

FRANK paced the waiting room floor as he'd done for the last—he checked his watch once again—four hours now. There hadn't been any word in over three hours, and to get that little bit of information, Frank had gone back to flashing his badge and scaring the crap out of half the hospital staff, but they knew nothing. Karl had gone home an hour ago, but he said he'd be back. Frank heard footsteps and expected to see Karl, but instead he saw Jim walking toward him, along with Luanne, one of the other agents. "How is he?" she asked, giving Frank a hug.

Frank knew how he'd acted at the warehouse must be all over the office by now and was probably halfway to Washington.

"No word. Last I heard, they weren't sure he'd survive the surgery. That was three hours ago, so I guess that's something."

Jim got up and walked to the nurse's station, returning a few minutes later. "He's still in surgery."

"That's good news, Frank. It means he's still alive," Luanne told him, and she actually took his hand. "We all heard what you said at the scene and I think it was sweet." Jim made a face, and Luanne elbowed him in the side hard enough that he grunted. "You know it doesn't matter to anyone."

Frank looked at her in disbelief, only to be proven wrong when he heard more footsteps and other agents began arriving. They all joined him in the waiting area, and thankfully Luanne took on the role of communications director and made sure everyone knew what little there was to know. "We're all here for you and Les. He's a great guy," an agent from one of the other teams that Frank didn't really know told him. Frank looked around and realized just how much he'd dismissed all these people, and here they were when he needed them. Damned if he wasn't a complete fool.

Over the next few hours, people from the office came and went, sitting with him and talking about nothing. But at least it made the time pass. Karl came back and sat with him as well. "Harvey said he'd be up later this evening. He's taking care of Koshigawa and his men. It seems they're having trouble finding a lawyer. Word got around that one of the people he tried to rip off was Brian Watson, and the attorneys that like him won't touch the case, and those that dislike him don't want to face him as a witness." Karl suppressed a bit of a grin. "They may need to go to Madison to find one, not that we really care." Karl grew quiet and settled on the sofa next to him. Others continued to arrive and leave, and all the while Frank grew more and more impatient.

Frank felt completely helpless, but to his utter surprise, he wasn't alone. Colleagues from the office that he barely knew stopped by and asked about Les on their way home. They all knew what he was going through and they all showed their support, and it touched Frank's heart. But that wasn't all that had touched his heart.

Frank looked toward the nurse's station as he thought and worried about Les. He'd touched his heart, there was no doubt about that. If Les made it, Frank had no idea what they were going to do, and if he didn't.... Frank swallowed and closed his eyes tightly, willing the tears that threatened to go away. He could not cry here in front of all these people, but his heart ached and the tears were so close. "Agent Jennings," a voice said over all the others, and Frank looked up from the chip in the floor tile he'd been staring at, a tear he couldn't stop rolling down his face. "I'm Dr. Piero, the surgeon who operated on Mr. Carlton."

"Is he alive?" Frank asked, his voice breaking.

"Yes. It was very touch and go for a long time, but he is alive. We have him in intensive care and he'll be there for a while, I'm afraid. He's asleep right now and he'll remain that way for at least twenty-four hours. His body has been through a lot. The bullet hit a number of organs, and I believe I was able to repair the damage, but he's very weak. And quite frankly, with that much internal damage, he's lucky to be alive at all at this point." The doctor took a deep breath, and Frank held his. "The next two days will tell the tale for him. There's nothing more anyone can do for him now." The doctor turned to the room. "I suggest you all go home and get some rest." The doctor turned back to Frank. "We'll call you if anything changes."

"Can I see him?" Frank asked, and the doctor nodded.

"For just a few minutes," the doctor agreed. "See the nurse on duty, and she'll take you back.

The others began drifting out of the waiting room, saying their good-byes, and after they'd gone, Frank walked to the nurse's station, and she asked him to follow her. She led him back past beds and monitors before quietly pushing a curtain aside.

Frank swallowed and gasped when he saw Les lying on a bed, tubes attached to him, with one down his throat. He looked pale and so small. Frank moved around to the side of the bed and took Les's hand, his thumb running along the back. Carefully, Frank brushed his hand over Les's forehead, soft hair passing beneath his palm. "If you can hear me, you need to fight and come back to me." Frank heard the nurse leave, and he continued holding Les's hand and talking to him softly until the nurse returned and told him his time was up. Frank took a last look and then turned away, leaving the area and heading back to the waiting room.

Harvey stood up as Frank walked into the room. "How is he?"

"Asleep. He was hurt very badly. He made it through the surgery, but they don't know anything beyond that." Frank sat on one of the sofas and prepared to get comfortable for the long haul.

"We've got Koshigawa and all his men in custody. Shelley is currently matching the bullet they took from Leslie with the guns from the scene to see who fired the shot," Harvey explained, and Frank nodded, not really comprehending much by this point. "Go home, Frank. You need to get some rest. You can't do him or anyone any good if you're dead on your feet." Frank shook his head. "That wasn't a suggestion," Harvey said firmly. "I can promise you that any change in his condition will be reported to me and to you."

Frank nodded, too tired to argue with Harvey, not that it would do him any good, anyway. Getting to his feet, Frank walked toward the elevator, with Harvey right behind him. They rode down together, and Harvey followed him to his car, probably to make sure he actually left. "Thanks," Frank said before getting into the car and driving home on autopilot.

In the house, Frank walked into the kitchen and pulled out a container of mint chocolate chip ice cream, eating out of the container before shoving it back into the freezer, turning off the lights, and walking up the stairs. His feet directed him to the room Les had been using, and Frank walked inside, sitting on the edge of the bed. Les's suitcase sat open on the chest at the end of the bed and Frank picked up a rumpled shirt from on top. Les had worn it, and Frank could smell his musky scent on the fabric. For some strange reason, it made him feel closer to him. Getting up, Frank held on to the shirt as he walked to his own bedroom.

Sitting down to take off his shoes, Frank looked at the bare white walls, the only decoration the blue draperies on the windows. Frank always thought he liked things minimalist, but now the room seemed cold and sterile. Still holding the shirt, Frank realized he didn't even have any pictures of Les. They were too new, and things were too undefined. Staring at the walls, Frank imagined pictures of the two of them with their arms around each other's waists, smiling at the camera. That was what he wanted with Les—to have a life together complete with happiness and memories. Frank sighed to himself and set the shirt aside. Stripping off his clothes, he climbed beneath the covers and set the shirt near his pillow before closing his eyes and doing his best to fall asleep.

FRANK knew he must have dozed off at some point in the night, because the room was suddenly light, but he hadn't slept much, not that it mattered. He got up and showered quickly before shaving and dressing so he could head out the door. Not bothering to check the time, he was surprised when he looked at the clock in the hospital lobby and it wasn't even seven o'clock yet. As he headed for the elevator, a man stopped him and said that visiting hours hadn't started yet, but Frank flashed his agency identification and continued on his way. At the desk outside ICU, he approached the nurse and showed her his identification. "Can you tell me anything about Mr. Carlton?"

"No, I'm afraid not."

"Do you have his personal effects?" Frank knew he should have thought about them yesterday, but he simply hadn't been thinking at all.

"Just a minute," she answered, and she returned with a small envelope. Frank opened it and pulled out Les's cell phone and began sifting through the numbers.

"Thank you," he said and carried the envelope to the waiting area before dialing the number he wanted.

"Hello, Leslie, honey," a female voice said, and Frank realized with a start that no one from Les's office had thought to contact his mother. Either that, or no one had contacted Les's superiors. Frank made a note to speak with Harvey.

"Mrs. Carlton, my name is Frank Jennings with the FBI, and I'm working with your son in the US."

"What's happened? Is he all right?" She'd gone into instant concerned-mother mode.

"No. I'm afraid he's not. Les was shot yesterday and right now he's in intensive care. He's had surgery and he made it through the night, but he hasn't woken up yet. I'm sorry it took so long to call you, but...."

"Janette, get on the phone and charter a plane to, Milwaukee, is it?" It took Frank a second to realize she was talking to him again.

"Yes, ma'am," Frank confirmed.

"Milwaukee," she said away from the phone, "and I want it ready to leave as soon as possible." Then he heard the phone shift again. "Have the doctors said anything to you?" Frank could hear her fear and concern come through the phone.

"Not yet this morning, but I'll track them down as soon as I get off the phone and call you once I have an update," Frank offered, but he heard no response initially. For a second he thought they'd lost their connection.

"Of course," she answered. "I'll be expecting your call." The connection ended, and Frank slipped the phone into his pocket as he inhaled a deep, steadying breath. He wasn't sure what he'd been expecting when he'd called Les's mother, but he was glad he'd called. She deserved to know what had happened to her son, and she deserved to be here if she wished.

"Agent Jennings," a nurse said as she approached, "it's still early, but I'll take you back to see Mr. Carlton."

"Has there been any change?" Frank asked as he turned to follow her.

"His vital signs are stronger this morning, which is a good sign, but I can't tell you any more than that. The surgeon was just with him and he's waiting to see you." The nurse led him down the same hallway he'd seen the night before and to the same location in the ward. Les looked the same except he seemed less pale. Frank wasn't sure if maybe he was seeing what he wanted to see.

"If his breathing continues to improve, we'll be able to remove him from the respirator soon," the doctor said softly from behind him. "He's doing better than I thought was possible. We're keeping him sedated for now so he doesn't try to fight the treatment, but once we remove the intubation, we'll reduce the sedatives and try to bring him around."

"You're hopeful, then," Frank said as he took Les's hand.

"Guardedly, yes." The doctor gave him a quick smile and then moved away.

Frank found a chair next to the bed and settled into it, still holding Les's hand. "I talked to your mother, and she's on her way," Frank told Les quietly. "You weren't kidding when you said she was a bulldog. She had her assistant booking a charter flight before we got off the phone." Frank swallowed hard as he watched Les's chest slowly rise and fall. "Get better and wake up, Les. I have so much I want to tell you. So many things I think I've figured out, and so much I want to say to you." Standing up, Frank leaned over the bed and lightly kissed Les's forehead before leaving the area and walking out of the hospital. He placed a call to Mrs. Carlton but left a message when he got voice mail, then shoved his phone back into his pocket.

He drove to the office and parked in his usual space before swiping his badge and riding up in the elevator. "How's Les?" Karl asked as soon as Frank reached his desk.

"The doctor says he's doing better," Frank answered before motioning that he needed a minute and walking to Harvey's office. "Did you call Les's superior in London?" Frank asked as he walked into the office.

"Of course. Why?"

"They never notified his mother," Frank told him, a touch of anger boiling inside him. "She's on her way, and I got the impression that she'll be here as fast as humanly possible." Les's phone rang, and Frank pulled it out of his pocket. "Hello, Mrs. Carlton," Frank said. "Les is doing better. They're keeping him sedated, but he wasn't as pale and his vital signs are stronger."

"Thank you," she said, sounding a bit relieved. "We're leaving shortly."

"Call when you're on the ground, and I'll meet you and take you directly to the hospital," Frank said, and he watched Harvey's eyes widen as he disconnected the call. "She's chartered a plane and is already on her way. I'd hate to be Les's superiors when she gets her hands on them."

Harvey smiled briefly. "I need your report as soon as you can get it to me. Koshigawa's found an attorney who's trying everything he can to get his client out on bail. And as soon as that happens, he'll hightail it to Japan and we'll never see him again."

"I'll get that to you soon," Frank said and walked back to his desk to get started on the paperwork. He completed his report and sent it to Harvey before wandering down to the lab with Karl to see what progress had been made.

"Got him," Shelley exclaimed as Frank walked into the lab.

"Got who?" Frank asked, and Shelley beamed at him.

"I found Koshigawa's prints on the case with the money. He's been claiming that the case wasn't his, but I have his prints on it and on some of the money. The man is going down!" Shelley lifted her gaze from her screen. "How's Leslie doing?"

"He was better this morning. His mother is on her way from London to see him." Frank could not get Les off his mind no matter what he did or who he talked to, and even Shelley wasn't an exception.

"Go on," Frank heard Shelley say as she swatted him on the shoulder. "You haven't heard a word I said, but that's okay. I won't take it personally. We've got enough on Koshigawa to put him away for a while, and he's not getting away," Shelley reassured Frank as she pushed him toward the door. "Get your work done and go see your man."

Frank stopped moving. "You really don't mind?"

"Why should I?" Shelley put her hands on her hips, and Frank knew he was in trouble. "I've known you were gay since the day you walked in here, and my feminine wiles did nothing for you. You're the only man here who looks me in the eye first rather than my chest, so yeah, I knew you were gay. Big deal. Most of the other guys don't care, either. This isn't 1950, and those attitudes have no place here, anyway. So you go see Les, and if he wakes up, give him a hug for me." Shelley turned back toward her computer and the room full of lab equipment.

"I will," Frank promised and hurried out of the lab and up to his desk. Frank worked with Karl, and they spent most of the rest of the day laying out their case and making sure everything was ticked and tied. It was. As Shelley said, there was no way Koshigawa was getting out of this one.

Frank's phone rang after lunch. "Agent Jennings, this is Anne from St. Luke's Hospital. Mr. Carlton is beginning to wake up." Frank whooped and nearly dropped the phone.

"Sorry," he said, and he heard the nurse chuckling on the other end of the phone.

"It's perfectly all right."

"I'll be right up." Frank hung up the phone and grabbed his things before running for the elevator.

"Where are you going?" Harvey asked as he came flying out of his office.

"Les is waking up," Frank explained as he pushed the call button. "My report is in your inbox, and Karl has all the evidence laid out and ready to go. Shelley is finishing the ballistics and forensics." The elevator door opened and Frank held it, waiting for Harvey's approval.

"Go on. You won't be worth shit the rest of the day, anyway." Harvey smiled briefly, and Frank bounded into the elevator. As the doors closed, he willed the car to move faster before racing out the door as soon as it opened.

The drive from the office to the hospital was made in record time, with lights and sirens. Frank pulled out all the stops, and he arrived on the floor out of breath as the nurse motioned him back. "He's a little groggy, but he was asking for you. That is if you're," she said, snickering, "Snuggle Buns."

"I'm going to kill him," Frank said as they walked into the ward.

What met Frank's eyes were Les's deep blues staring back at him from behind the tubing. "They'll be taking the tubes out soon, but until then he can't talk." Frank saw a small pad on the table with barely legible scribbles on it.

Frank looked at her and nodded before turning back to Les, who looked miserable, his eyes pleading at Frank from behind the thing down his throat. "Get word to his doctor that we need that tube out as soon as possible." The nurse nodded, and Frank saw Les's gaze soften in its intensity. Frank sat next to the bed and took Les's hand, stroking his skin, sending a silent but unmistakable message that he was there and he was staying with him. The nurse returned and the doctor followed.

"You'll need to step out," the doctor said to Frank, but Frank stared back at him and shook his head, daring the doctor to contradict him. The doctor capitulated, saying, "Okay," before turning to Les. "We need to pull this out, and you need to be as still as you can. Your gag reflex will kick in, and you can help by trying to curb it for us." The doctor turned to Frank. "You can help by keeping him from moving."

Frank continued holding Les's hand, placing the other firmly on his shoulder as the doctor got everything prepared and then slowly pulled out the tube. Les began to cough, and the doctor moved slightly faster. After a few seconds, the tube was out and Les settled back on the bed, breathing on his own. The nurse handed Frank a glass of water with a straw, and Frank held the straw to Les's lips. "Just a small sip, sweetheart," Frank said, and Les took a sip before closing his eyes in pain.

"Just relax your throat. I know it's sore, but that will fade. How is the pain otherwise on a scale of one to ten?" the doctor asked, and Les swallowed again, his eyes closing, but his expression less pain-filled.

"About a seven," Les croaked, and Frank could tell Les was doing his best not to move at all.

"We'll give you something for it, but you're probably going to be sleepy," the doctor explained, and Frank watched as the nurse inserted a syringe into the IV. Within a few minutes the pain lines around Les's eyes began to fade. "Feeling better?" the doctor asked, and Les nodded slightly, his head settling back on the pillow. "Rest now." The doctor patted Les's arm and left the area. The nurse fussed around Les's bed for a few minutes, checking tubes and monitors before leaving as well.

"Did you really call me sweetheart?" Les asked in a raspy voice. "I heard you say it when I was shot and I thought I dreamed it."

"You didn't dream it," Frank answered as he stroked Les's hand. This felt so right. Not the part about Les in a hospital bed, but the part where he was there for Les, comforting him, holding his hand. That part felt amazingly right.

"Oh. You're my sweetheart too," Les said as his eyes closed.

"The nurse asked if I was Snuggle Buns."

"You're that too," Les answered softly. The medication must have really kicked in, because Les's features relaxed, and he looked for all the world like he'd drifted off to sleep. "Has anyone called my mother?" Les asked, keeping his eyes closed.

"I talked to her this morning, and she's on her way now," Frank explained before adding, "Harvey called your supervisors yesterday, but no one contacted her." Les's eyes opened, but he didn't say anything. "Needless to say your mother did not sound happy." Frank wasn't particularly pleased himself. "Rest for a while. I'm not going anywhere except to help your mother."

"She's going to love you," Les said with a slight smile before he closed his eyes, and this time Frank was sure that Les had fallen asleep. Les's phone vibrated in Frank's pocket a few minutes later.

"Hello," Frank said, getting up to leave the area, moving to the waiting room.

"Agent Jennings, this is Andrea Carlton. We just landed, and I have a car and driver. I don't need a lift."

"Les is in Intensive Care at St. Luke's. I'm with him now," Frank said. "He's awake, and while tired, he seems lucid and he's been talking to me. Right now he's asleep because they gave him some pain medication. I'll tell him you're on the way."

"Thank you," she said with obvious relief. "I'll see you soon." She hung up, and Frank put the phone back in his pocket and walked back to Les's bed. After sitting in the chair once again, Frank took Les's hand and felt Les tightened his fingers around his. Les's eyes fluttered open briefly before closing again. He didn't say anything, and it wasn't necessary. Frank held Les's hand and sat with him quietly.

"This is what I always wanted," Frank murmured softly, and Les's eyes opened briefly and then closed again. "Sleep." He hadn't meant for Les to hear him, but what he'd said to himself was true. Frank was content to sit near Les's bed and simply hold his hand. He couldn't think of anyone else he would be content to just sit with. Frank had too much energy, and he always seemed to be moving, but with Les he was content to just be. Getting comfortable in the chair, Frank closed his eyes as the lack of sleep and days of vigilance caught up with him.

A small gasp broke through his doze, and Frank opened his eyes. Les's mother stood at the end of his bed with her mouth open. Frank knew instantly who she was because she was the female miniature version of the man he loved. Frank nearly gasped himself as the thought came unbidden to his mind. "Are you Agent Jennings?" she asked in a surprisingly demure voice.

"Please call me Frank, Mrs. Carlton." He stood and held out his hand.

She shook it with a firm grip. "Andrea," she said, still staring at her son.

"He's been dozing for a while, but I think the medication has really kicked in." Les barely stirred. Frank offered her the chair, but she shook her head, and Frank sat back down, taking Les's hand once again.

"Where did you go?" Les murmured, and Frank felt his fingers tighten, but Les didn't open his eyes. Frank noticed that Andrea's eyes went to their clasped hands, but she didn't say anything about it.

"Your mother is here," Frank told Les, and he shifted slightly on the bed, his eyes sliding open for a few seconds before closing again. "I'll be right back," Frank told Les, and let his fingers slide out of Les's before placing his hand under the blanket. Then Frank stood and motioned for Andrea to join him. Looking at her, Frank could tell she had plenty of questions. They stepped out, and Frank led her to the waiting area.

"Have you eaten? We could go to the cafeteria for a few minutes. Les will probably sleep for a while."

"That would be nice, thank you," she answered, and Frank led them through the corridors and down to the cafeteria. They got in line, Andrea getting a small amount to eat and Frank doing the same, joining her at a table, waiting for her questioning to begin.

"Is he going to be all right?"

"The doctors are optimistic. He's awake, and that's a good sign. Hopefully all he needs now is time to heal." God, Frank hoped what he was assuming was true.

"You like my son." It wasn't a question. "I wasn't expecting to see you holding his hand. Not that I mind, it was simply a bit of a surprise. He didn't mention you to me."

"We're sort of new," Frank said because it was all he could think of. He wasn't going to try to explain things to her because he didn't really understand them himself. All he knew was how he felt, but now that the case was over, Frank suspected that Les would return home, and Frank knew he needed to keep his heart in check or he was in for a great deal of disappointment.

"Does he know how you feel?" Andrea asked with a slight smile.

"I believe so," Frank answered, a little uncomfortable discussing this with Les's mother when he hadn't had a chance to really discuss things with Les. Frank watched as Andrea sipped from her tea.

"You know I'm going to take him back with me," Andrea said.

"I figured as much." Frank felt his stomach drop, but he'd known that was going to happen as soon as he'd called Les's mother. "I want what's best for him." The thought of Les leaving again made Frank's vision swim for a few seconds, and he blinked a few times to try to keep the room from spinning. Frank hadn't thought he'd had any illusions about what would happen when the case was concluded, but they were there and they'd been shattered by Andrea in less than a minute. He had been hoping that Les would somehow be able to stay. Up until a few hours ago, Frank had been sure he was going to lose Les to the injuries, and now that it appeared he was going to recover, he was going to lose him to real life.

Frank returned his attention to the plate in front of him, but all he did was push his food around. His appetite had flown along with his hope. He should have known better. Once Andrea finished eating, Frank picked up both trays, placing them in the window for dirty dishes, and escorted Andrea back upstairs. When they entered, Les was awake, and Andrea walked to the bed, kissing Les lightly before sitting in the chair. Frank walked to the other side of the bed, lightly touching Les's arm. "I'll let the two of you talk." Frank felt his throat closing as he took a final look before saying good-bye. He nearly turned to leave, but stopped himself and leaned over the bed to kiss Les's cheek. "I'll see you soon." Frank left Les in his mother's capable hands and made his escape from the hospital before he completely embarrassed himself.

"I DIDN'T expect to see you here," Karl said from behind him, and Frank whirled around on the barstool a little too quickly and nearly fell off before steadying himself.

"I was looking for you," Frank answered, and he signaled to the bartender for another. Frank saw him shake his head. "Where were you, anyway?"

"Spending a quiet evening at home, until I got a call that the man I'd brought in the other night was sitting at the bar drinking himself into oblivion."

"I haven't had that much," Frank protested.

"Maybe not, but Jeremy was doing us both a favor," Karl said, and he motioned to the bartender, who gave each of them a cup of coffee. "So do you want to tell me why you're here instead of at the hospital with Les?"

"His mother arrived. He doesn't need me anymore."

"Come on, big guy, let's get you home." Karl tugged him off the stool, and Frank followed behind. He didn't think he needed any help, that is, until he nearly tripped over his own feet. Frank managed to make it to his car and gave Karl the keys. Settling in the passenger seat, Frank closed his eyes and let Karl drive him home. "Frank, we're there," he heard Karl say two seconds later, and it took his fuzzy brain a minute to realize that he must have fallen to sleep and Karl hadn't somehow magically transported them here while his eyes were closed.

Frank got out of the car and loped up toward the door, fishing for his keys, but he couldn't find them and so Karl opened the front door, letting him inside. Karl guided him up the stairs and into his bedroom. Frank didn't protest as his shirt and shoes were removed. The last thing

Frank remembered was a warm blanket and his pillow—everything else was a complete blur until he woke up and his mouth felt like he'd stuffed cotton in it, his head pounding.

"Serves you right for drinking like an idiot," Karl said as he placed a glass in front of him after Frank stumbled into the kitchen.

"What's this and what are you still doing here?" Frank asked as he curled his hand around the cool glass.

"It's a surefire hangover remedy, and I'm still here because I was concerned about your sorry ass. I can get a taxi back to my car if you're going to be a jerk," Karl said louder than was necessary, and Frank cringed.

"Sorry," he said and took a sip from the glass. It tasted god-awful, but Frank drank part of it anyway and almost immediately his stomach settled and his head began to clear. A second later, Frank was gasping for air as he rushed to get a drink of water. "What the hell is in this?"

"Tabasco," Karl answered as Frank gulped some water.

"Are you trying to kill me?" Frank gasped as he turned off the faucet.

"No," Karl answered levelly. "If I were, I'd have added more. Now go get showered, and we'll stop at the hospital on your way to work." Frank glared at Karl, but it didn't work. "Don't be an ass. You're going to go see him, and you're going to talk to him. The least you can do is be a man and tell him how you feel." Karl turned from the sink, placing his hands on his slender hips. "You butch guys figure you can muscle your way through everything, but sometimes all you need to do is talk." Karl walked closer. "Les deserves to hear how you feel and what you want. He can always say no, but if you don't ask, the answer is always no."

Frank shook his head but stopped as the room wavered around him. Straightening up, he stared down at Karl. "If you weren't my friend, I'd probably punch you in the mouth."

"Then it's lucky for you we're friends, because if you punched me in the mouth, I'd knee you in the balls. Never forget, we nerds fight dirty." Karl chuckled, obviously pleased with himself, before turning back to the sink and rinsing out the glass as Frank slowly began to climb the stairs.

Frank got undressed and stepped beneath the shower, the warmth invigorating him. Once he was clean, he brushed his teeth, scrubbing away the bad tastes from his mouth. After padding to his room, Frank dressed and began to feel normal, and by the time he came back downstairs, he felt as good as he could expect. "Do you need me to drop you at your house so you can change?"

"I'm off today," Karl said as he joined Frank in the hall. "Just drop me at home for my day of leisure. Well, more like laundry and grocery shopping, but you get the idea. Say, aren't you supposed to be off today too?"

"I guess, but I want to check on things with the case," Frank said, but he didn't think Karl was buying it.

"Fine. Drop me at my place, and I'll change and then ride to the hospital with you. Ya big baby. You can stare down men who want to kill you, but you'd think talking to the person you cared about was a death sentence."

"You're skating on thin ice," Frank said in his most menacing tone. Frank shook his head and grabbed his case from the hallway.

"Let's go," Karl said, rolling his eyes slightly. Obviously that tone didn't work on Karl anymore. Frank decided it was best to let Karl have his way. He really wanted to see Les; he just wasn't sure it was the best thing to do for either of them. Les was going back to London with his mother, and Frank would still be here. He didn't see a way around it. They walked to the car, and Karl threw Frank the keys. "You know I'm right," Karl finally said after they'd ridden in silence for a while.

"Maybe, but I don't know what good it will do," Frank said without looking away from the road. "He's leaving. I knew he would once the case was solved, and it is. Wanting something really bad doesn't change reality."

"Sure it does. Because if you want something, sometimes you can make it happen. It's always worked for me." Karl sounded too damned cheerful and pleased with himself to be healthy. "I wanted to work in the field, and no one ever thought I would, including Harvey, the man who could have given me an assignment at any time. But it happened, and I'd like to think I did well."

Frank couldn't stop his smile. "You did great. But it's not the same thing."

"Sure it is. But this time it starts with you talking to Les. Find out what he wants instead of just assuming it's what you expect." Karl turned to look out the window. "You might be surprised."

"Fine, I'll try it. But if it backfires, I'm shooting your ass!" Frank tried to sound menacing again, but all he got for his efforts was Karl's grin. "Damn it!" Frank swore, and Karl chuckled.

They pulled up to Karl's apartment building, and Karl led him inside. "I'll be a few minutes."

Frank settled on the sofa and looked around the room. It was surprisingly homey, with family pictures and even a throw on the back of the sofa that looked like it could have been made by Karl's mother. This was not at all what he'd expected. Somehow he'd expected a computer dungeon with servers and wires everywhere. "This is a nice place, Karl."

"Thanks. I'll be just another minute." Karl was true to his word, and soon they were on their way to the hospital. Frank felt more than a little nervous, but he did his best to hide it. At the desk, they inquired about Les and were told that he'd been moved to a room. "He isn't to have visitors yet," she added, but Frank flashed his badge, and she waved him past and told him where to go. It didn't take long for them to find Les's room, and Frank knocked quietly on the door before stepping inside.

"You look much better," Frank said when he saw Les's deep-blue eyes looking up at him. Andrea sat near the bed and looked up at him, smiling slightly. "Karl, this is Les's mother, Andrea Carlton." They shook hands.

"I'm going to get something to drink," Andrea said.

"I'll go with you," Karl offered, and he extended his arm. Andrea beamed and let Karl lead her out of the room. Frank heard them talking quietly as they walked down the hall.

Frank turned his attention to Les and took the chair Andrea had vacated. "How are you feeling?"

"Better, now that you're here." Les rolled his head toward Frank. "I was beginning to think you weren't going to come back." Hurt flashed in Les's eyes.

"I almost didn't. When you feel better, you'll leave again, and I figured it might be better if we made a clean break of it." Frank refrained from taking Les's hand even though he wanted to very badly.

"What changed your mind?" Les asked softly.

"Karl. He said I should talk to you about it instead of simply assuming I was right. I'm glad he pushed me to come. I wanted to see you as soon as I left yesterday.

Frank gave in to what he wanted, too, and took Les's hand, his thumb stroking the soft skin. "I didn't want to get hurt, but I realized that if I didn't take the chance, I'd be hurt anyway. You'd leave with your mother, and I'd have lost you. So here goes." Frank took a deep breath. "I want you to stay, Les. I want to see where we go from here. I want to go to sleep with you every night and wake up to you in the morning. I know I probably have no right to say anything like this, because I know I'm asking you to give up a lot, but I'm doing it anyway because I'm pigheaded and selfish and I know what I want." Frank looked into Les's blue eyes, watching his expression closely, but Les gave him no indication of what he was thinking. "I'm asking a lot, and you don't need to give me an answer right away. Hell, I understand if it's too much and you need to go back, but I didn't want you to leave without knowing how I felt."

"How do you feel?" Les asked. "If you only tell me once, just be honest with me and say it." Frank felt Les squeeze his hand. "I know it's hard for you, but tell me just once what I mean to you."

Frank swallowed hard and thought about how he'd felt when he'd seen Les with a bullet wound in his side and when he'd thought Les might die. "You mean everything, Les, because I love you." Frank lowered his face to Les's hand and lightly kissed the warm skin.

Frank felt Les rest his other hand lightly on the top of his head. "I love you too, Frank. The thought of leaving hurts pretty badly. My mother offered me the position of head of store security here in the states if I want it," Les said, and Frank looked into his lover's eyes. "She's been trying to bring me into the company for years."

"Is that what you want? Because you'll only come to resent me if you take the job only to be with me. If you're not going to be happy...."

"Hey. I like my job, but I've been thinking about doing something a little less dangerous. I've always known I would someday have to work for my mother. She started the business, and it's my legacy. So, yes, I can start there, and we can see what happens." Les's eyes danced for a few seconds, and Frank leaned over the bed, bringing their lips together in a gentle kiss. Frank could hardly believe what Les had told him, and he couldn't stop the smile that burst onto his face as soon as they broke their kiss.

"Karl is never going to let me live this down," Frank mock-groaned, and Les chuckled before wincing slightly.

"Don't do that," Les said. "I'm injured, remember?" He yawned widely, and Frank watched as he closed his eyes, a slight smile on his face. Frank continued holding Les's hand as his lover fell asleep, and he sat like that, unwilling to break his touch with Les until Andrea and Karl returned.

"Is he asleep?" Andrea asked, and Frank nodded. He moved to give up the chair, and Les tightened his grip. Frank saw Andrea smile. "I take it you two had a talk." Frank nodded. "And I also take it he's decided to accept my offer."

"That's up to him," Frank explained, and he felt another squeeze of his hand.

"You never told me if we got Koshigawa," Les said without opening his eyes.

"Yeah," Karl answered, "we got him. He's fighting us every way he can, though. We now have a team of lawyers to deal with, and they've refused to let us anywhere near him and his gang. They even called in favors from the Japanese embassy."

"He'll do that until you break him," Les murmured. "Koshigawa is not about to give up as long as he has something to lose. Unfortunately, he has a way of wearing everyone down until they simply don't want to deal with him anymore."

Anger coursed through Frank, and he let go of Les's hand. Koshigawa was responsible for Les getting shot, and he was not going to get away with it. Reaching into his pocket, Frank pulled out his phone. "That's not going to happen this time." Leaning over the bed, Frank gave Les a kiss on the forehead. "I've got some things to do, but I'll be back this evening." After saying good-bye to Andrea, he and Karl left the hospital room.

"Where are we going?" Karl asked as they stepped into the empty elevator.

"To try and finish what we started," Frank answered as the doors slid closed, and he began dialing.

TWO hours and a number of phone calls by both Frank and Harvey later, Frank sat in a secure video conference room, along with Harvey, listening to a low-level state department flunkie named Welch tell them why they couldn't do what they wanted to do. "The Japanese are screaming bloody murder over this. They want to see the evidence that Koshigawa's guilty. They claim we entrapped him, and you want us to request access to his home on Japanese soil. There's no way they'll agree." The bureaucrat looked smug.

"We understand it's difficult, but we have solid evidence," Harvey said in a conciliatory tone—the same tone he'd been using throughout the entire useless meeting.

Harvey began to say something more, and Frank overrode him, standing up and walking right in front of the camera. "Listen here, you cotton-brained paper pusher. We have Koshigawa dead to rights on this one, because I'm the one he tried to buy stolen goods from, and I saw his men shoot our Interpol partner on this case. So you listen—I don't care how mad the Japanese government is about this. You work for the *American* people, and Koshigawa has a number of works of art in his collection stolen from American citizens and sheltered under Japanese law. The Japanese cannot hide their heads in the sand any longer, because we have proof that he's been buying stolen goods, so therefore everything in his collection is suspect." Frank took another step closer, his face becoming larger on the screen. "You realize that we aren't going to be able to keep this quiet."

"You were ordered not to speak to the media," the man on the monitor countered impatiently.

"Yes, I was, but you have no control or authority over our Interpol partners, and they will be speaking to the media. I can tell you there will be plenty of good old-fashioned Midwestern anger when it comes out that the US State Department would rather side with the Japanese than American taxpayers and voters who are the victims here." Frank could see beads of sweat forming on the diplomat's brow.

"There are more things at play here than just this one case," the diplomat explained levelly, but Frank could see the frustration in his eyes.

"I don't really care," Frank responded with a sharper edge to his voice. "I expect you to put pressure on the Japanese government to open Koshigawa's collection to the FBI and Interpol so it can be determined just how much stolen art he has. With the evidence we have, there is no way he can claim he was an innocent purchaser, and if we're right, there are wealthy and powerful people in this country who will be grateful."

"There really isn't anything that we can do," the diplomat said as if he were speaking with a child having a temper tantrum.

"Then, Mr. Welch, be prepared for some fallout, and I'll make sure your name is spelled correctly." Frank pressed a button on the table, cutting off the connection. He heaved out a breath and turned to Harvey, who smiled.

"You were perfect."

"Do you really think it'll work?"

Harvey grinned. "Of course. He's shaking in his boots because the last thing he wants is his name in the papers. He'll call by the end of the day, and we'll get most of what we want." Harvey stood up and walked toward the door. "Go on back to the hospital and give Les our best."

"I will," Frank said with a smile before getting Karl and leaving the office.

AFTER dropping Karl at his apartment, Frank went back to the hospital. He was surprised when he walked into Les's room and found the bed gone and the room empty. His heart skipped a beat. Telling himself that Les was probably down for tests, Frank walked to the nurse's station.

"Can you tell me where Mr. Carlton is?" he asked with as much patience as he could muster.

The nurse consulted her records. "He's down in surgery," she answered. "I'm not at liberty to discuss his condition any further."

Frank reached into his pocket and pulled out his shield. "You are now. Tell me what happened."

The nurse's eyes widened. "He was having pain and swelling, so the doctors took him right down to surgery. The surgical waiting room is on the first floor." Frank thanked her and headed toward the elevator.

He found Andrea fidgeting in the waiting area. "He's going to be fine," she said as soon as she saw Frank. "They just came in and said he's in recovery. They missed a small internal bleeder and they went back in to fix it. At least that's how they explained it to me." Andrea seemed as worried as any parent would be, and Frank sat down next to her. "He began to scream, the pain got so bad, and everyone rushed into the room. They had him down to surgery within ten minutes." She dabbed her eyes with a tissue. "I really thought I was going to lose him."

"Mrs. Carlton," the attendant at the desk said to them quietly, "Mr. Carlton is awake, and they're moving him back to his room."

"Thank you," she answered before standing up. Frank did the same and offered her his arm, which she accepted.

"After you see him, you should get some rest," Frank told her, and she nodded her agreement, even though Frank could tell it was the last thing she wanted to do. "I'll be happy to take you back to your hotel."

When they arrived in the room, Les was waiting for them, looking groggy but awake. At least he didn't have a tube down his throat this time. Frank brought a cup to his lover's lips and Les drank a little. "You gave me a real scare," Frank told him with a slight smile to take the edge off his worry.

"Sorry." Les took another sip of water, and Frank set the cup on the tray. "Are you still going to want me once I'm covered with scars?"

Frank leaned close and whispered in Les's ear. "I'll want you no matter what. I want you now, but you've been a little busy. So you need to get better so I can *show* you how much I love you rather than just tell you." Les nodded slightly and closed his eyes with a definite smile on his face.

"I'm going to take your mother back to her hotel so she can rest. I'll be back later once you've had some sleep." The only indication Frank got that Les heard him was a slight nod as he fell asleep. Andrea kissed her son good-bye, and then Frank escorted her out of the hospital and to his car. After dropping her at the Pfister, Frank continued home and was making himself a light dinner when his phone rang. "Hello, Harvey."

"They caved. State is going to do what they can. It seems they now see the benefit of our argument. We'll have to wait and see what happens now."

"Thanks, Harvey. Les went back in for surgery but he's out now, and hopefully that's the last scare and he'll start to heal."

"Let's hope so," Harvey said, and Frank agreed with him wholeheartedly.

CHAPTER 8

LES was going stir-crazy. He'd been out of the hospital for a week now, and Frank continued to fuss over him like a mother hen. Granted, it was nice to be taken care of. Les's mother had gone home a few days ago, and Frank had moved Les into his house to recuperate. Les was still on leave from his job, and since he'd been injured while working, he wanted to make sure he was covered before resigning. His mother had offered him a number of potential positions, and Les figured he'd have to decide on one soon.

The front door opened, and Les heard Frank's footsteps in the hall. "What are you doing down here?" Frank asked lightly. "The doctors said you still need to take it easy."

"Going down the stairs once is not strenuous exercise," Les argued, but he stopped when Frank kissed him and groaned when Frank pulled away. "Where are you going?"

"To hang up my coat and start dinner. Why?"

"I have something else in mind," Les countered. "You haven't touched me since I got home from the hospital, and when I saw the doctor yesterday, he said I could resume limited normal activity."

"So…," Frank prompted.

"Limited normal activity includes you fucking me," Les said as he unbuttoned the light shirt he was wearing and let it fall to the floor.

"Who says?" Frank said, but Les watched him swallow and saw Frank's eyes widen with definite interest.

"I do." Les walked up the stairs, and he could feel Frank's gaze on him. At the top, he slipped off his pants, giving Frank a good view of his ass before stepping into the bedroom. Lying on the bed, Les only had to wait a few seconds before he heard Frank racing up the stairs. Frank stopped at the bedroom door, and their eyes locked.

"I don't want to hurt you," Frank whispered even as he took off his shirt and began to strip out of his pants.

"You won't hurt me if you're careful," Les countered and watched as Frank stepped out of the last of his clothes. Les motioned him over, and when Frank stepped closer, Les curled a hand around his lover's length, swiping his thumb over the weeping head. He heard Frank's throaty moan. "Do you really want me to stop?"

"Les," Frank whined, and he thrust into Les's hand. "More action, less talking."

Les put his lips to better use, tugging Frank closer, encouraging the bigger man to straddle him on the bed before sliding his lips down Frank's long, thick shaft. God, he tasted good—and felt good. He'd missed Frank so much, missed the intimacy of a lover. Frank rocked slightly, and Les relaxed his throat and took Frank deep before holding him there.

Frank's moans turned into near frantic cries of joy, and Les bobbed his head, feeling Frank slide his hand through his hair before lightly cupping his head. "God, I missed you," Frank told him, the love, lust, and passion clear in his voice.

"I missed you too," Les said as his lips slid away, and Frank settled on the bed next to him. Les climbed on top of his lover, and Frank kissed him hard, his cock sliding along Frank's hip. "I wasn't sure you wanted me anymore. You didn't touch me even though we slept next to one another for days." Les looked into Frank's eyes, trying to get his lover's honest reaction.

"I'll want you when we're both old and gray. Never doubt that," Frank told him as he brushed strands of hair out of his face. "You are the most amazing man I've ever met, and I have no intention of letting you go. I also will not hurt you if I can help it, and you just got out of the hospital."

"A week ago." Les ground his hips against Frank's, reveling in his lover's reaction. "Do you have any idea how hard it was, pun intended, to sleep beside you and not have you touch me?"

"Yes, I do," Frank answered as he slipped his hands down Les's back to cup his butt, then kneaded Les's cheeks with his strong fingers, "because it was just as hard for me. But I will not hurt you." Frank growled before taking Les's lips in an almost harsh kiss that left Les breathless and panting.

Frank slid his fingers down Les's crack, and Les whined, pressing back into the touch. "I want you, Frank."

"I know, sweetheart." Frank slipped a finger inside Les's body, and Les threw his head back with a long, deep groan. "How about you ride me?" Frank asked him, and Les nearly whooped before moving to straddle Frank's body. Taking the condom Frank handed him, Les opened the package and slid the condom down Frank's length. Slicking up himself and Frank with the bottle of lube Frank handed him, Les slowly sank onto Frank, sighing at the slow, filling burn. "Yes…." Les drew out the word until Frank was buried deep inside him.

Les stilled and let his body adjust to the mind-blowing sensations that seesawed through his body like a whip. Then he braced his hands on Frank's chest and slowly began to move.

"God, you feel good," Frank moaned, and Les smiled at his lover, taking him deep within his body. Les had been dreaming of this for days. He'd thought of taking matters into his own hands while Frank had been at work, but the anticipation and banked desire he felt now were more than worth the wait. Holding his body still, Les gave control over to Frank, who drove up into him like a madman, hitting that spot with blinding accuracy. Les's body thrummed as he tried to keep control of himself, every motion of Frank's body driving Les closer to passionate insanity.

Frank caressed Les's legs, and Les's muscles began to twitch and shake with excitement. "Missed this," Les gritted out between clenched teeth as he tried to keep his body under some semblance of control. Frank was hitting all the right spots in all the right ways, but Les did not want to come yet. He was already dangerously close, and then Frank lightly ghosted his fingers over the mark from his surgery and Les lost it, gushing his release onto Frank's chest. Gasping for air, Les felt Frank drive deep before throbbing inside him as he cried out his own climax.

The weakness that had been so near the surface since the shooting, and that Les had thought was behind him, returned with a vengeance, and he collapsed onto Frank's chest, where he gasped for air. "Breathe," Frank told him softly, but Les could hear concern in his voice.

"I'm okay." Les took a deep breath and released it slowly, lifting his head to look into Frank's eyes. "You took my breath away. You always do."

Frank smiled. "I'm the only one you let do that?"

"You're the only one who ever could," Les corrected lightly before lowering his head to Frank's shoulder, his lover slowly caressing his back. This was how Les wanted to feel forever. He was loved, there was no doubt about that. It had happened so fast, and Les was simply grateful that they both seemed to understand what it meant and were willing to grab and hold on to it.

"So beautiful," Frank murmured softly, and Les smiled, snuggling closer and letting Frank's warmth lull him into a light doze. "Sweetheart," Frank whispered. "I hate to say this, but we need to get up."

Les lifted his head, glaring at Frank in mock agitation. "Why? I'm happy right here."

Frank chuckled softly. "We're going to stick together, for one thing, and we have someplace we need to go."

"We do?" Les searched his brain, trying to remember if he'd forgotten anything.

"It's a surprise, and I think you're going to like it."

"As much as I liked what we just did?" Les teased.

Frank's eyes clouded and he cupped the back of Les's head, carding his fingers through that long hair. "I hope not." The searing kiss wiped away the notion that anything could ever be as good or as special as what he and Frank had together. It simply wasn't possible. Frank gently rolled onto his side, settling Les back on the mattress. "You're damned amazing."

"So are you."

Frank gave him a final kiss and then climbed off the bed, padding naked to the bathroom. Les waited until he heard a flush before gingerly following. Pushing open the door, he walked to where Frank stood at the sink, looking in the mirror. Without a word, Les pressed his chest to Frank's powerful back, his arms wrapping around Frank's waist. "I always hated being pale and never getting a tan."

Frank shook his head and brought Les's arm up to his chest. "Look how amazing we look together, your translucent skin against mine."

"Yeah, my ghostly white against your rich olive," Les said sarcastically.

"Look how good we look together," Frank repeated, and Les rested his chin on Frank's shoulder, happy and contented. Les admitted to himself that they did look and feel good together. This was right— Les could feel it down to his toes. Les wasn't perfect, and neither was Frank, but Frank was perfect for him. Turning in Les's arms, Frank kissed him softly. "We need to go or you'll miss the surprise." Frank left the room, and Les did his business before washing up. Returning to the bedroom, he dressed and stepped gingerly down the stairs. "Are you hurting?"

"No. Just being careful," Les answered as he stepped into the entrance hallway. He wasn't being completely truthful. After their earlier exercise, Les was feeling a bit sore, but it would pass.

Frank held the door for him, and Les walked outside for what seemed like the first time in months. The evening air had a slight hint of autumn to it as Les walked to the car. Getting inside, he waited for Frank to lock the house, and then they were speeding through town, heading south along a road where Les could catch glimpses of Lake Michigan between the houses. Traffic got heavier as they got closer to downtown, and Frank wove around before parking in front of the building where the two of them had first met. They got out of the car and walked toward the front door.

"Mr. Temple," Frank said as they met him halfway up the walk, "I was so pleased to get your call, and I thought Les could use some time out of the house. He's doing much better." Frank turned and smiled at him. "He had us really worried there for a while." Frank turned back to the other man. "What can we do for you?"

"Well, I know it sounds petty in the light of what happened, but I was wondering when we would get the windows returned?" The school administrator seemed rather nervous.

"Hopefully very soon," Frank explained. "We have a court hearing in a few days, and we'll petition the judge to let us return the windows. I don't think he'll object."

"Good. Thank you. Would you like to come in for a cup of tea?" Mr. Temple motioned toward the front door, and they stepped inside.

Les saw Frank look up the stairway and Les followed his gaze and halted in his tracks. Pink and white dogwood petals clung to branches on a field of radiant blue across three large panels, the light of the setting sun through the glass casting a beatific glow. Les felt a tingle run up his spine as goose bumps formed on his arms. "Is this my surprise?"

"Yes," Frank answered. Neither of them could take their eyes off the stunning Tiffany glass.

"They were reinstalled this morning, and I called Frank. We all wanted you to be the first to see them since you were the ones who got them back for us," Mr. Temple said with a huge smile, and Les realized that his little subterfuge from earlier was what had made him seem nervous. "Go on up," he encouraged them, and Les carefully walked up the stairs, standing on the landing as the sun illuminated the windows. Frank stood next to him, and they stared at the masterpiece in glass before walking back down the stairs.

"Thank you, Mr. Temple," Les said. "I'm glad we were able to get them returned."

"The students put together a celebratory concert to celebrate their return," Mr. Temple explained.

"Let us know when it is so Frank and I can be sure to attend," Les said.

The school administrator walked to the large set of doors and pulled them open. "Right now."

Les was floored when he saw a large group of children, some as young as five and others who might be in high school or college. Two chairs sat in the center of the room, and Mr. Temple motioned them forward. He and Frank took their seats, and Mr. Temple motioned the youngest children to come forward on the stage. The youngsters smiled and played a short little song on their instruments, and once they were done, he and Frank clapped as loudly as two people could. Then older children came forward, each group playing an increasingly complex piece of music. After each piece, Les clapped until his hands hurt, feeling incredibly honored. When they were done, Les stood and thanked all the kids, and it was their turn to break into applause. In all his life, Les had never had anyone applaud for him.

The children then surged forward, laughing and joking with each other. "Are you a real FBI agent?" one of the younger boys asked Frank.

"Yes," he replied, reaching into his pocket and pulling out his badge. A lot of the boys crowded around so they could see it. "Les is an Interpol agent. They're like the European FBI."

"Did you really get shot?" another boy asked. He must have been about eight.

Les lifted his shirt and showed the boy the scar on his side. "The bullet went in right there."

"Cool!" the boy responded with wide eyes. Les knew the wound was many things, but he wasn't sure "cool" was one of them. However, he didn't argue with the youngster as he tucked his shirt back in.

"All right, there are refreshments out back on the lawn," Mr. Temple said, and all the children filed out in a raucous group after the near-deafening sound of instrument cases being snapped closed. "Their parents will be here in about half an hour," Mr. Temple told them. "You both did a great thing for us. Thank you."

"You're very welcome," Les said, knowing he was speaking for both of them. "It was our pleasure to help."

Frank thanked the administrator for everything, and they left the school, walking toward the car. "Have you ever been more appreciated for doing your job?" Les asked, watching Frank over the top of the car as he walked to the other side.

"No, I don't think so," Frank answered thoughtfully before opening his door. Les got into the car as well, fastening his seat belt as he waited for Frank to start the engine. "But I can think of some other ways to make you feel appreciated," he nearly purred.

"I bet you can," Les responded before leaning over the seat. Frank met him halfway, and what began as a light kiss quickly escalated into something much more heated. "How about you take me home and prove it to me," Les said, and Frank zoomed into traffic with a determined look on his face.

$\mathcal{E}$PILOGUE

FRANK unfolded his legs and got out of the tiny car, standing at the edge of the lawn of a large home with glass walls, the sound of water flowing over rocks reaching his ears. Everything about the building and the grounds spoke of tranquility, quiet, and money—lots of money.

Les got out as well, but the look on his face was much less appreciative. "This is my last official act as an Interpol agent," Les sighed.

Frank turned toward his lover in concern. "Are you really okay with that? It has to be hard to have that part of your life end." He'd been concerned about Les ever since he'd handed in his resignation and began working for his mother. Outwardly, Les seemed to enjoy it, but Frank wanted to make sure the man he became more and more convinced each day was the love of his life was truly happy.

"New challenges," Les answered. "Sure, it's hard to walk away, but I have challenges I never dreamed of. Besides, I spend my days doing what I always did, trying to figure out who is full of shite and who's telling the truth, same as I did before. Only now they're not necessarily criminals, just executives with their own objectives." Les turned and grabbed the laptop bags from the backseat, handing Frank his. Closing the car door, they walked up the stone path. The front door opened, and a man stepped outside, bowing politely.

Frank bowed as well before extending his hand. "Mr. Tanaka," Frank said, and he smiled, and they shook hands. Then Mr. Tanaka shook Les's hand as well.

"I want to restate our agreement with your governments. Nothing is to be removed from Mr. Koshigawa's house now, but those items you can prove are of questionable origin will be tagged and arrangements will be made to return those items to their rightful owners," Mr. Tanaka said before he turned and escorted them toward the house.

"We understand and are willing to abide by those terms. You have seen our databases?" Frank asked.

"Yes. And the government of Japan is willing to accept that any items definitively matched to the items in your databases should be returned to the owners listed in your databases. You have been most cooperative," Mr. Tanaka said formally.

"As have you," Les replied with a slight bow, and Mr. Tanaka led them inside the house. They took off their shoes in accordance with Japanese custom and placed them by the door. Frank could not help marveling almost as soon as he crossed the threshold. The home was simplistically elegant in design, with screens and traditional Japanese room divisions. But it was the items in the rooms that took Frank's breath away: art from almost every culture and period of history. "Where can we set up?" Les asked, his voice nudging Frank out of his thoughts to more practical matters.

"I have arranged for this room to be available for your use. I am surprised there are not more of you."

"They will be here tomorrow. We thought it best to start carefully," Les explained. When Frank had been approached to undertake this job, he'd insisted on Les coming along, and Interpol had agreed to let him act as their representative in this matter. Hearing Les with their Japanese counterpart, Frank knew he'd made the right decision. Les had patience, and Frank could already feel himself getting anxious to begin, so he kept quiet and let his partner do what he did best.

"I thought you would like to begin in here." Mr. Tanaka led them through to the back of the home and opened the door to a large room that glittered with the glass from dozens of windows, all Tiffany and each a masterpiece. "There are more in panels that recess into the walls." Mr. Tanaka walked to what looked like tall cupboards and slowly pulled out what appeared to be a long door. Another window mounted in frame glided out of the wall.

"I'll go get the laptops," Frank said, hurrying back to the room to see Les staring at one of the windows. "What is it?"

"This is the window that started it all. The one that put me on Koshigawa's trail almost a decade ago," Les explained before turning away. After setting the computers on a small table, Les booted up and connected to the Interpol stolen art database. It took him seconds to bring up the window in question. Frank watched as his lover tagged the item as located and inserted the appropriate information.

"You are efficient," Mr. Tanaka said with a nod and a slight smile. "This helps prove your suspicions were right." Frank could tell, even on the practiced diplomatic face of Mr. Tanaka, that he'd been hoping they were wrong.

He and Les spent the rest of the morning reviewing all the windows in the room, and they were able to identify almost a dozen pieces that had been stolen from the United States and a few more that had gone missing in Europe. Tomorrow they would have the rest of the team review their work. After lunch, an interesting experience, since Frank had no idea what he'd actually eaten, they began on the next room, and Frank noticed that Les stopped in his tracks.

"Holy God!" Les said, staring at the painting on the wall. "That's a Monet, and it's been missing for almost twenty years."

"Let's get it cataloged," Frank said, and he watched as Les stepped closer before opening his laptop. Setting it down on the floor, Les began typing frantically, and Frank watched and waited, wondering what he was up to. Once he was done, Les turned the computer so Frank could see it.

"This painting has been missing for two decades. The reason I know it is because it's a bit of a legend in art circles. I won't go into the story right now, but remind me later over a bottle of wine. Let me just say that while everyone believed it had been stolen, no one ever connected Koshigawa to it."

Frank stepped to Les, his excitement drawing Frank like a moth to flame. "Did you ever think you would be here and have the chance to actually go through Koshigawa's collection?"

Les stopped what he was doing. "Not in my wildest dreams. Why do you ask?"

"Because the only reason we're here is because of you. A lot of people are going to get items they thought were gone forever returned because of you."

"Because of us," Les said before adding, "we make a great team."

"That we do," Frank agreed, "but in this case it was all you. We recovered the windows in Milwaukee and would have returned them to the conservatory without looking any further. You are the most amazing man I have ever met, and because I met you, I looked deeper and found the connection that would return you to me and brought us here. This artistic pursuit is all because of you." Frank saw Les lean toward him. "We can't, not here," Frank said remorsefully before leaning closer. "But when I get you back to the hotel," Frank lowered his voice, "you are going to make love to me until we both scream." Frank stopped and waited. He knew the moment Les realized just what Frank had said.

"Are you sure?" Les swallowed hard, and Frank nodded slowly.

"There's a first time for everything, and I want it to be with you. You're the first person I've loved enough or trusted enough." Frank grew quiet and nodded. "I love you more than I can possibly say."

Les's radiant smile lit the room. "I love you too." Les stared at him for a long while, until they both heard Mr. Tanaka's footsteps outside the room.

"Now, sweetheart, we need to get back on task and find out how much more of this art we can get returned to its rightful owners," Frank whispered with a smile before they both returned to work.

ANDREW GREY grew up in western Michigan with a father who loved to tell stories and a mother who loved to read them. Since then he has lived throughout the country and traveled throughout the world. He has a master's degree from the University of Wisconsin-Milwaukee and works in information systems for a large corporation. Andrew's hobbies include collecting antiques, gardening, and leaving his dirty dishes anywhere but in the sink (particularly when writing). He considers himself blessed with an accepting family, fantastic friends, and the world's most supportive and loving partner. Andrew currently lives in beautiful historic Carlisle, Pennsylvania.

Visit Andrew's web site at http://www.andrewgreybooks.com and blog at http://andrewgreybooks.livejournal.com/. E-mail him at andrewgrey @comcast.net.

Also from ANDREW GREY

ANDREW
GREY

LEGAL
ARTISTRY

http://www.dreamspinnerpress.com

Also from ANDREW GREY

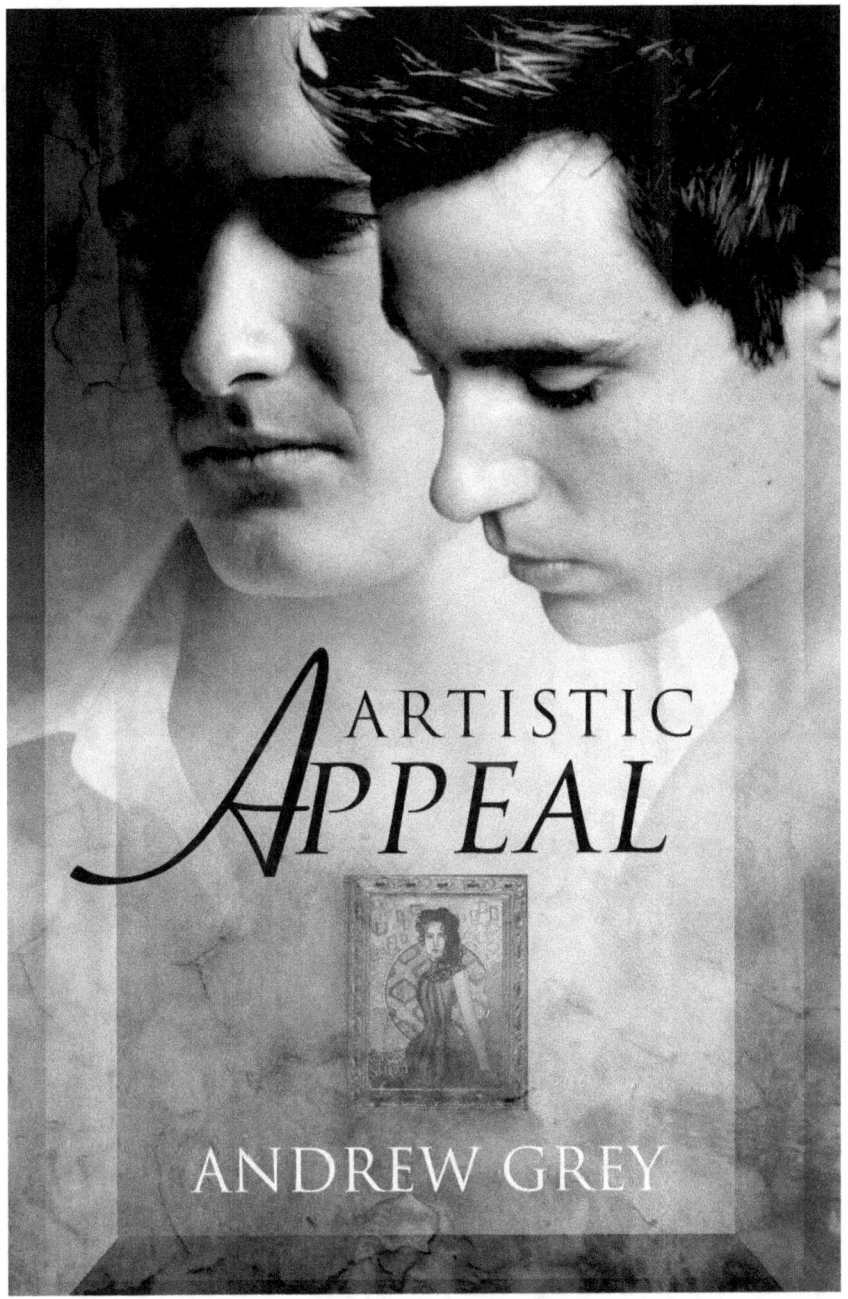

ARTISTIC
APPEAL

ANDREW GREY

http://www.dreamspinnerpress.com

The LOVE MEANS... stories by ANDREW GREY

The LOVE MEANS… stories by ANDREW GREY

http://www.dreamspinnerpress.com

The BOTTLED UP stories by ANDREW GREY

http://www.dreamspinnerpress.com

STORIES FROM THE RANGE by ANDREW GREY

http://www.dreamspinnerpress.com

Contemporary Romance by ANDREW GREY

http://www.dreamspinnerpress.com

Contemporary Fantasy by ANDREW GREY

Also from ANDREW GREY

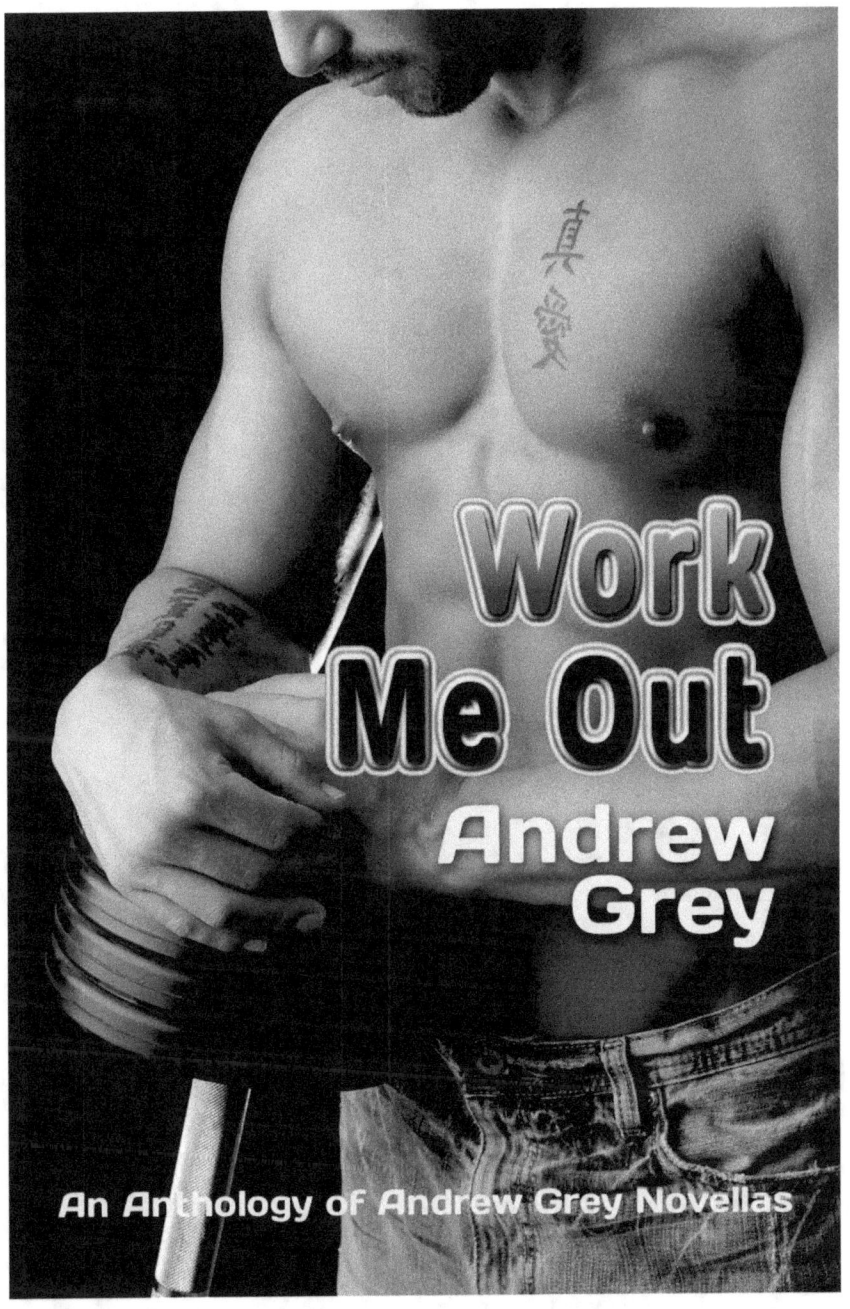

An Anthology of Andrew Grey Novellas

http://www.dreamspinnerpress.com